LEFT AT OZ

A Jennie Connors Mystery

LEFT AT OZ

•

Sandra Carey Cody

AVALON BOOKS
NEW YORK

Published by Avalon Books,
an imprint of Thomas Bouregy & Co., Inc.
160 Madison Avenue, New York, NY 10016

Library of Congress Cataloging-in-Publication Data

Cody, Sandra Carey.
  Left at Oz / Sandra Carey Cody.
    p. cm.
  ISBN 978-0-8034-7664-6
  I. Title.
  PS3603.O296L44 2011
  813'.6—dc22
                          2010046202

PRINTED IN THE UNITED STATES OF AMERICA
ON ACID-FREE PAPER
BY RR DONNELLEY, BLOOMSBURG, PENNSYLVANIA

*To Pete, my husband, my best friend,
and an unfailing source of encouragement—
and to my sister-in-law, Carolyn Stebbins,
who loves all things* Oz

Acknowledgments

Writing for Avalon makes me part of a very special group of writers. Whatever our genres, we share a belief that "happily ever after" is possible and that good will triumph over evil. Thanks to the wonder of the Internet, many of us have become friends, though we have never met face-to-face and our physical addresses span the globe. I am truly thankful for the encouragement given me by my fellow Avaloners.

Chapter One

*L*eft at Oz. Jennifer Connors stared at the words scribbled on the envelope back. Could she have misunderstood? *No. They said Oz. Definitely Oz. I didn't get everything, but—*

Kate's voice interrupted. "So, how'd Tom take the news?"

"I didn't tell him." In answer to Kate's sideways look, she added, "Why worry him? It'll all be over by the time he gets back."

"Face it, Jen. We won't find it. Chances are a zillion to one."

She's wrong. It's going to work out. Jennie believed that. Things almost always worked out. She kept this to herself, not wanting to be reminded how slim were their chances of finding the car. "If we don't look, they're a zillion to zero," she added.

There was another skeptical glance from Kate, which Jennie ignored, focusing instead on the parklike perfection of the streets they drove through. It was late August. Marigolds and zinnias flourished and sprinklers worked overtime to prolong the technicolor hue of Bermuda grass lawns. The only sounds in the car were the steady thrum of the engine and the raspy, teasing voice on the radio, assuring them it was "All for Love," buoying Jennie's natural optimism and coaxing a smile from Kate. They drove on like this until they reached the highway, the ease of their friendship such that silence was not uncomfortable. At the intersection Jennie looked again at the crumpled paper. *"West to River Road, then north."*

Almost immediately, they were beyond the subdivisions and shopping malls that sprawled outward from Memphis, intruding further each year into the Tennessee landscape. Wide, flat expanses of bottomland, planted in corn, stretched before them.

When they turned onto River Road, Jennie sat up straighter and kept an eye on the odometer. She felt a buzz of excitement as it registered the twenty-sixth mile. "Okay, it should be coming up soon," she said, and within minutes, "Slow down."

Just ahead was a white farmhouse, framed by a profusion of flowers, growing not just in the beds around the house but also in tree stumps, old tires, washtubs, and every kind of container imaginable. In front, a low fence sagged under the weight of a pink rambler. An elderly woman, tall and as graceful as the blooms that danced around her, was in the yard moving among the bright patches of color.

Jennie's hands beat a triumphant tattoo on the dash.

Kate's look in response was a *What? Are you nuts?*

"Don't you see?" Jennie said. "Cornfields. Everything's gray and dusty. Then suddenly there's color. That's Oz."

"Maybe." Kate didn't sound convinced, but she slowed down. "So, what next?"

Jennie studied her list. *"Left at Oz,"* she read. "That could mean they left the car at Oz." She looked past the yard and the farmhouse to the outbuildings in back. "Or it could mean turn left. There's a crossroad just beyond the house."

Kate said, "Well, we can't very well search that lady's barn. I vote we turn left."

The woman had stopped her work and was watching them.

They turned onto a narrow road lined with tall trees stretching up through brushy undergrowth. Occasionally a break in the foliage provided an area of mottled sunlight. Further down the road, the open areas disappeared. Trees inched closer until, finally, branches reached out and interlaced, turning the space through which they traveled into a vaulted tunnel.

Jennie leaned forward, peering into the woods on first one side and then the other. Her head just missed the windshield when the car jolted to a stop. "Jeez!"

Kate pointed to the huge black oak towering in front of them. "End of the line."

Jennie looked around, discovered a weed-choked road on the left. "What about that?"

"It's private property."

"How do you know?"

"There was a house before that last bend." Kate spoke in that tone that comes when patience is stretched thin.

"It was just a shed."

"Someone's living there."

Jennie refused to listen. "Everything on the tape was right so far. It must be around here."

"You really want to go on?"

"We've come this far. Why stop now?"

"Okay"—Kate puffed her cheeks and blew out the air—"but it's shank's mare from here."

"Leave the car?" Jennie's courage ebbed. She willed it back. "What the heck. I didn't spend all those weekends with the Girl Scouts for nothing. Lead the way."

"You lead the way. I never did the Girl Scout thing."

On foot, they followed the road, little more than a path, about a hundred yards before it took a sharp turn to the left. The woods ended abruptly after the bend. Jennie blinked, momentarily blinded, when she stepped from the shaded area into the light. There it was—the 2002 Taurus, heat waves shimmering off its dark red surface.

She moved forward, refusing to acknowledge the tremor that passed through her. "I knew we'd find it." She half turned and saw that Kate was no longer following. "Come on. If the keys are there, I'll drive to the police station."

"You can't do that." Kate seemed planted where she had stopped.

"Why not? Don't you want to see that cop's face when I show up with the car?"

"What about fingerprints? That kind of stuff?"

Jennie strode forward, dismissing Kate's concern. "Who cares?"

"That cop. He'll care."

Jennie didn't look back. She drew a wayward courage from Kate's fear. "I have my car now. Why should I send some kid to jail?"

"You're feeling sorry for a thief?"

"A thief with a conscience."

"It didn't keep him from stealing your car."

"He called. Told me how to find it." She ignored the butterflies doing the limbo in her midsection until she reached the car. "It'll be okay." The assurance was as much to herself as to Kate.

She opened the door, and then stumbled back, retching. She put her hands on her knees, struggling to remain upright, and closed her eyes, but she had already seen too much: a delicately formed body in the space between the seats; a hand twisted at an unnatural angle; an outline of cheek and chin, turned away from her, but still visible; hair the color of pale honey, matted with a dark substance. *Blood.* She knew it was blood.

Chapter Two

At the police station, Jennie gripped the edge of the counter with both hands. On the other side of the glass partition, a noisy printer claimed the attention of a stocky young woman. Jennie leaned forward, reading the small plastic rectangle clipped to the woman's pocket. "Ms. Dugan?"

The woman looked up, seemingly surprised to hear her name. "What can I do for you?"

"I need to talk to Sergeant Smith." When there was no reaction from Dugan, Jennie added, "I'm Jennifer Connors. My car was stolen yesterday. He's the officer I talked to."

"Hey, Smitty," the woman called over her shoulder. "Somebody here to see you."

Smith was smiling when he came forward. "Heard you tried to get in touch with me." There was an almost imperceptible change in his expression when he came close enough to see Jennie's face. "I got your message. Tried to call you back, but you weren't home. Haven't found your car yet."

"Is there some place we can talk?"

"Sure. Come on back." He opened the door at the end of the counter, allowing them to pass through, and led them along a row of metal filing cabinets. Jennie felt the stares of everyone in the room as she and Kate followed Smith through the maze of scarred, mismatched desks. Her tan Bermuda shorts and pink T-shirt had seemed fine when she'd set out this morning. Now, clammy with perspiration, they clung to her, adding to the feeling of exposure. She held her head high and directed her gaze toward the far wall. A large patchwork tote bag slipped off her shoulder and swung from her arm, striking her leg each time she took a step.

If Theodore Smith noticed anything unusual, he gave no sign. He continued to talk as he escorted the two women toward the back of the room, his voice soft and amiable.

"Can I get you anything? Cup of coffee? Maybe a doughnut?"

Nothing like the surly, picture-perfect cops seen on TV, Smith was balding and overweight, and possessed the courtly manners of the Old South. Jennie was glad she would be telling her story to him instead of one of the younger men. When they reached a desk near the wall, he cleared a stack of papers from the straight-back chair at its side and held out his hand, offering the chair to Jennie.

She sat and was quiet for a moment, fixing in her mind what she must say. Finally, still avoiding eye contact, she forced herself to speak. "We found the car."

Without comment, Smith leaned over the cluttered desk and selected a folder from the stack he had removed from the chair. When neither of the women spoke again, he cleared his throat and prompted, "You found the car . . ."

"There's more." She paused for another deep breath, and added, "I mean I have more to tell you." She began to speak, aware that the only sound in the room, other than the rustling of paper, was her own halting voice. Somehow she found the words she needed. She told him about the message, finding the car, about the body, and other things, details she had not been aware she knew. She related all of this as if in a trance, oblivious to the activity beginning to boil around her.

"The hands, they were—" She looked down at her own hands. "Dainty. Made me . . ." Her voice drifted. She continued to look at her hands. Something made her think of her children, but she would not say that, could not bring herself to mention their names in this place.

This morning, just a couple of hours ago, seemed like a different world. The big oak table in the sunny alcove of her kitchen's bay window—that was real. Two little boys with straw-colored hair— that was her world. Neither of them had finished their breakfast. *They'll be okay,* she told herself, and tried to believe it. With the perversity of the very young, they were exhilarated by the news of the missing car, much too excited to eat, especially Andy, the six-year-old.

"Wow!" he said, "Nothing like this ever happened to us before!"

Tommy, practical beyond his eight years, wanted to be sure he had every detail exactly right. He asked more questions than Sergeant Smith had, while Andy, unconcerned with details, made a mess of his cereal, chopping at the floating banana slices, arranging the pieces into the shape of a gun, and spinning a tale of stolen cars and heroic cops.

Jennie struggled for patience and lost. "Andrew, stop it. Don't play with your food. And I don't want to hear another word about guns."

Thinking back, she wished she'd been more patient, but she hated guns, hated the violence and ugliness they represented, hated, most of all, that she could not shield her sons from it. Now, this—

"We'll finish in the car."

Startled by an unfamiliar voice, she looked up. A tall, almost skeletal man loomed over her. She vaguely remembered Smith waving his arm and the other man joining them.

"Come on," the tall man said, slicing the air with his pen and moving closer.

She saw his shadow on the floor and moved her feet beyond its reach.

"Who are you?" she asked.

"Lieutenant Weston Goodley Homicide."

That was the way he said it, all together, so that homicide sounded like part of his name. He was younger than Sergeant Smith—probably in his mid-thirties, and much thinner, clearly not a man to waste time on doughnuts and squad-room pleasantries.

They were in a car now. A police car. A van with RIVER COUNTY printed in heavy black letters on its side followed them. Sergeant Smith was driving and Lieutenant Goodley was sitting in the front seat with him, half-turned so that he faced Jennie and Kate in the back.

We're going to the scene of the crime. Words from a movie. But this was real life. Her life. Impossible.

Goodley's strident, nasal voice persisted. "The hands reminded you of something."

She thought a minute, trying to remember. "A bird," she finally said.

"The hands reminded you of a bird?"

She nodded.

"Why a bird?"

"I don't know. They just . . . I don't know."

More questions, the same questions, over and over, until Jennie's answers became rote, and her thoughts began to drift.

The hands. She kept coming back to the hands. She thought again of her kids. It was as if she were two people: One, she heard speaking, telling what she had seen. The other was standing beside the car as the door swung open. Seeing. Turning her face so that she would not see. But still . . . seeing. She could not stop seeing. *Hands.* One was twisted, crushed. And more. *No.* She would not think about that. *Think about something good. Tom.* She drew strength from the mere imagining of how it would feel to have his arms around her. If she could just lean into the comforting solidity of his body, tuck her head under his chin, and inhale the warm, clean scent of him. *Hurry home, Tom. Please hurry.*

"Okay." Goodley interrupted her thoughts. "Let's go over this again. What did you do after you left here yesterday?"

"Well, after we got home—"

"How'd you get home?"

"My cousin picked us up."

"Cousin's name."

"Ellen Deighton."

Good old Ellen, Jennie thought. *How many times has she rescued me?* It had been Ellen who stood beside Jennie in their grandparents' rose garden eleven years ago. "Please, Ellen," Jennie had coaxed. "I know it's sudden. But sometimes it happens that way." She'd reached out both hands and added, "He's the one. And you introduced us. I'll never forget that." And then, without waiting for an answer, she'd let go of Ellen's hands and spun away in a twirling, giddy dance, too full of her newly discovered love to think of anything except the wonderful fantasy her life had become.

"The message . . . ," Goodley said. "Tell me again how it led you to the stolen vehicle."

Stolen vehicle. Jennie shrank from the words. That was the beginning. *That's what led me to . . . Don't think about it. Just tell him about the message.* That was easy. It was before her as a scene in a movie: Her finger pushing the button on the answering machine. Listening. Not understanding. Listening again.

"At first I thought it was just noise," she told him. "Then I realized there was music. Loud. Really blasting. Everything was distorted. It took me a minute to realize someone was talking. I heard the word 'car' and I played the message again. Several times, in fact. Finally I picked out more words, a few phrases. I never got all of it."

"Tell me what you did get."

Jennie didn't need the crumpled paper to repeat the words she had listed. They played in her head, an intrusive litany: *Car. River Road. North. Twenty-Seven miles. Cornfields. Left at Oz. You deserve. Her too.*

"That's it?"

"That's all I could make out."

Goodley drummed his fingers on the seat back and listened, never taking his eyes off Jennie's face. "From this you knew someone was telling you how to find your vehicle?"

Kate interrupted, "Can't you—"

A sharp look from Goodley silenced her.

Jennie continued, "With the loud music and all, I figured the message was from a kid. Sergeant Smith said kids probably took the car for a joyride, and then left it when it ran out of gas. He said they do that. I thought maybe one of them felt bad and called."

"And those few words were enough to direct you to your vehicle? From Memphis all the way up here to River County?"

"Well, when I heard River Road, I thought, 'Barney's is on River Road.' We'd been at Barney's. It seemed worth a try."

She was still trying to explain how the strange message had led them to the missing car when she saw the farmhouse. "There it is." She pointed. "Oz."

Goodley looked out the window and back at Jennie.

She tried to explain, but he continued to stare at her, impassive.

No imagination, she thought, and then softened, remembering Kate didn't get it right away either.

When they came to the crossroad, Jennie told Smith to turn left.

Goodley's droning voice began again. "Explain to me once more what you were doing in River County yesterday."

"We were at Barney's."

"By 'Barney's,' you mean Barnstable's Flea Market & Bar B Q Shack?"

She nodded. "We were shopping at the flea market."

"You come up here often?"

Jennie had turned to look at the van following them and didn't hear the question.

Goodley repeated it.

Kate interrupted, "She's told you all this a dozen times."

He ignored Kate and kept his full attention on Jennie. "Tell me again about the voice on the tape."

"It was—" She hesitated when she felt the police car slow down and then stop.

"This must be the big tree they told us about," Smith said, "and the dirt road." He checked the rearview mirror when he turned into the small lane. "Not sure the van can get through. Some of these branches are pretty low."

Goodley leaned forward, looked at the road, and then turned and looked past Jennie, out the back window toward the van. "How far is it?"

"Not far. Up ahead . . . you can just see light through the trees . . . the road veers left, kind of doubles back . . . right after that, there's a clearing. That's where—"

He got out of the car before she could finish. "We'll leave the vehicles here and walk the rest of the way." He motioned to the two men following in the van.

"Come with me," he said to Jennie. He turned to Smith. "You stay with her in the car." He indicated Kate by tilting his head in her direction. To the other men, he said, "Got everything?"

Both nodded. One held up a small black case with scuffed corners.

They walked single file down the old road with Goodley leading the way. The only sound was the crunch of last year's leaves under their feet. Within minutes, they reached the place where the trees ended.

In the center of the field Jennie saw the maroon Taurus, exactly as she had left it: front door still partially open, its bright surface garish and ugly against the soft golds of the meadow grasses. A cloud of flies hovered around the open door. She choked back the bile rising in her throat.

Goodley stopped about thirty feet from the car and, when he held up his hand, the others stopped too.

Jennie stood with the two men, watching Goodley. A concentrated energy seemed to flow from him when he moved forward. He pulled a handkerchief from his pocket and held it to his face as he walked around the car several times, looking at it from every angle, even lying on the ground to examine the underside. Next, he turned his attention to the area around the car, crisscrossing the space repeatedly, pausing several times to nudge a pile of leaves or a stick with his foot. Finally, he made a slow circle, surveying the open area and the surrounding woods. The cloud of flies parted when he took the handkerchief away from his face and reached into the car.

Jennie watched, fascinated and repelled.

He wrapped the cloth loosely around the steering wheel and tugged at it, gently at first, and then vigorously. He reached under the front seat, brought out a set of keys, and held them aloft. They rotated slowly, caught a slant of light, and sent it in Jennie's direction.

"These yours?"

She nodded.

"You leave them there all the time?"

"Not all the time. Sometimes. I hide them under the seat so I don't have to dig for them." Unconsciously, she shifted her shoulder under the weight of the tote bag.

"Okay," he said, "let's get this over with."

She remained motionless until he started to take her arm. She knew what was expected of her. *Identify the body. That's what he wants me to do.* Evading his touch, she moved closer to the car, stopped an arm's length away. *I can't do it. I won't.*

Goodley was at her side, watching her, his face expressionless. She didn't need to look. Even with her eyes averted, she saw it all too clearly. The image of the hand flashed in her mind. On and off. First the twisted, lifeless thing pushed against the seat, then the hand covered with droplets of water, demonstrating a swimming stroke.

She forced herself to say it aloud. "It's Robin. Robin Langley." She admitted this to herself for the first time.

"You know her?"

"Yes, she—" Jennie stopped midsentence, struck silent by a memory: Robin reading a story to Tommy and Andy, lamplight spilling onto three heads bent over a book, Robin's in the middle, her hair as corn-silk fair as theirs.

Chapter Three

Goodley was ominously quiet on the ride back to the station. When they pulled into the parking lot, he said, "I need a statement from each of you."

Jennie said, "I've told you everything I know."

"You want to call an attorney?"

"That's not it. Our kids'll be getting home from school."

His expression said she wasn't going to win this one. She went for a compromise. "Can Kate go?" she asked. "Somebody has to be there when they get off the bus."

He hesitated.

She plunged ahead. "I can give my statement, and then call someone to pick me up. Maybe you can wait until tomorrow for Kate's?"

"I'll drive you home when we're finished. I have to get that answering machine tape anyway." He turned to Kate. "I'll talk to you then."

"I live right next door to Jen." With that, Kate fled in the direction of her car.

The building Jennie thought of as the police station actually housed all of River County's government. It was a squat rectangle, constructed of concrete block, apparently with no thought for aesthetics; the walls, both inside and out, were painted the same murky beige. Exterior walls emerged from the macadam of the parking lot without benefit of shrubs; a double door was centered in the front wall. Just inside the door, recycled church pews were pushed against the front wall, providing the only seating in the narrow waiting area. Four feet farther in, a waist-high counter ran the length of the room. A glass partition extended upward another two feet from the counter, separating workers on the other side from lay visitors. Beyond the partition, clusters of desks represented the various branches of county government. Cubicles along the back and side walls served as offices for department heads. Agencies responsible for local taxes, road maintenance, and social services occupied the front two-thirds of the room. The police department, district attorney and coroner's offices were tucked away in the back, like unruly cousins whose existence was acknowledged only when occasion demanded.

Goodley led Jennie to his cubicle in the back right corner of the cavernous room and instructed her to sit down. He placed a tape recorder in the center of his desk and spoke into it, stating his name, the date, time, and location. Then he turned to her. "Mrs. Connors, this conversation is simply for the purpose of gathering information to help us in the investigation of a crime. No charges are being brought against you. However, if you wish to have an attorney present, you may call one. Do you?"

Jennie interrupted. "No."

"Are you aware that this conversation is being recorded?"

"Yes."

"And you consent to that?"

She nodded.

He pointed to the recorder. "You have to answer out loud."

"Sorry. Yes, I consent."

"Okay. Let's get started. State your full name and address please."

"Jennifer Gardner Connors. Eighty-five Magnolia Court, Memphis. That's in Rolling Hills. It's one of the northern—"

"I know," Goodley said curtly. "Age?"

"Thirty."

"Marital status?"

"Married."

"Occupation?"

"Well, I guess Activities Director at Riverview Manor. It's a retirement center and nursing home."

"You guess?"

"What I meant is that I haven't actually started the job yet. I'm supposed to start next week. The day after Labor Day."

"Are you presently employed?"

"Not really employed. I've been volunteering for several years. Just a few hours a week. But this year, since both of my children will be in school all day—"

A chopping motion of Goodley's hand cut her short. "The address of this facility?"

"I don't think there is a street number. It's on River Road, just past God's Grace Methodist Church."

"Can you tell me the name of the female who was found dead in your car?"

Jennie's voice faltered, but she managed to get the name out. "Robin Langley."

"Your relationship to Robin Langley?"

"She was a lifeguard and swimming instructor at our community pool. Sometimes she babysat my kids." Jennie bit her lip. "Could I get my purse? I need—"

Goodley took a tissue from the box on the corner of the desk, handed it to her, and asked, "How long had you known her?"

She blew her nose, regained partial composure before continuing, "A couple of years. The family lives in our neighborhood, just around the corner from us. We've known them since they moved there."

More questions. Endless questions, it seemed to Jennie. About Robin, the car, the taped message, and her listing of the intelligible portions of the message, until her head was spinning and she felt weightless, as though she were floating above the scene, observing a woman who looked and sounded strangely like herself.

"You still have those directions you wrote down?"

She gave him the crumpled envelope.

"Describe the voice again."

"Well, it was really strange, but . . ."

"What?"

She hunched her shoulders.

"You think it was someone you know?"

"I don't know. It didn't occur to me to wonder about that at the time. I just thought it was a kid imitating a cartoon character or something. That's what it reminded me of. A cartoon."

"Male or female?"

She spread her hands and looked up at Goodley, who was striding back and forth on the other side of the desk. "I can't say for sure. It was real high-pitched. Not a normal voice, either male or female. Maybe if I listen to it to again."

"Okay. We'll leave it at that for now. Let's get back to the flea market. Who knew you were going there?"

"A lot of people. All last week at the pool—"

"This the pool where Robin Langley worked?"

"Yes. Our community swimming pool. It's the neighborhood gathering place in the summer. Mothers talk while we keep an eye on our kids. Last week, since it was the week before school started, we were all talking about what we planned to do the first day of school. I said I wanted to get ready for my new job. I was looking for records with music from the thirties and forties. Someone suggested that I look at Barney's."

"Someone? Could you be more specific?"

She thought a minute before she shook her head. "The group kept changing. People came and went. You know, like people do. And everybody talks at the same time. I don't remember who said what."

Goodley sat down now and looked hard at her before he went on. "About the flea market. What did you do while you were there?"

"I shopped. Like I said, I was looking for old records."

"Were you with . . . uh?"

"Kate. Her name is Kate Britten."

"Were the two of you together the whole time?"

"Most of the time. Not the whole time. I took quite a while looking through the records, and Kate went off to do some shopping of her own."

"Did you talk to anyone else during that time?"

"Well, there was this old Englishman. He gave me his card." She looked through the voluminous tote bag and handed Goodley a cream-colored business card with EDWARD PYNCHON—DEALER IN OLD BOOKS & RECORDINGS engraved on its face. "We talked quite a while. He offered to look through the records he had stored somewhere and call me if he found anything."

And again, endless questions—about the most minute details of the past two days, until, finally, Goodley said, "Okay, that's all for now," and switched off the recorder. "I'll take you home and pick up that answering machine tape."

Driving home, the quiet in the car was oppressive, broken only by crackling sounds from the radio. Neither Jennie nor Goodley attempted conversation. She slumped in her corner as far from him as possible, listless until the car turned into the familiar driveway and she saw the kids, hers and Kate's, come out of the house next door, followed by Kate.

"Mom, where were you? Who's that guy? Is he a cop? Where's the car? Kate said you went to get the car." Tommy's questions came faster than Goodley's had. And Jennie was even less ready for them.

"I haven't told them," Kate said.

"Told us what?" demanded Tommy.

"In a few minutes," Jennie said. "Right now I'd like you to go back inside with Kate." She looked at her friend, who nodded. "You can watch TV. I'll be over in a little bit and we'll talk."

Andy was sizing up Goodley, who stood to one side watching.

"Are you a cop?" Andy asked him.

"Yes, I am," Goodley said.

"Did you find our car?"

"The car has been located."

"Where is it?" Andy was almost dancing with excitement.

"Andy," Jennie interrupted, "go with Kate. I'll be there as soon as I can."

Kate said, "Come on, guys. Your mom'll be along in a few minutes." She turned to her own children and said, "Trevor, Amelia, you come too."

Tommy started to object. "But, Mom—"

"Now!"

The eight-year-old gave his mother a quick look, and then went with Kate across the narrow strip of lawn separating the two houses. Andy turned to Goodley one last time. "Can I see your gun?"

"Andrew!"

Jennie bent to pick up the smoke-colored cat who snake-danced around her ankles when she opened the door, but he scooted away and crouched under a tall wing chair, pausing only to hiss at Goodley.

"He's funny about other people in the house," she explained to the police lieutenant, "but he usually isn't this bad."

"The answering machine," Goodley reminded her.

"It's over here." She led him to the desk. "Looks like there's a couple of new messages. I'll listen to them. Then you can take the tape with you."

There was a message from Sergeant Smith returning Jennie's call, and then Tom's voice. "Hi, Jen, it's me. I'll be home tonight about ten. That's assuming the plane's on time. Surely by eleven. See you then. Tell the troops I miss them. Love you." Next there was a click, and the time: 1:33.

"That's my husband," Jennie explained. "You can take the tape now."

"I'll listen to it here first. I want you to listen too. See if you can identify the voice."

She pushed REWIND. The machine started to whir.

"Your husband on a trip?"

She nodded. "A business trip. Seattle."

"When did he leave?"

"Two days ago. Sunday."

The whirring of the machine stopped. Jennie pushed PLAY. They heard Smith's brief message, Tom's voice again, "Hi, Jen . . ."

"Those are the only messages on the tape," Goodley said. His mouth was a straight, severe line.

Jennie rubbed her forehead, thinking, trying to remember every detail of the previous evening. "I hope I didn't erase it." Her voice was little more than a whisper, but it was enough to shake Goodley's icy mien.

"You don't know?"

"Well, I don't think I did, but . . . I can't be sure. You know . . . things like that, you do automatically."

"Didn't you know how important it was?"

"Not last night. How could I?"

"You knew your car had been stolen."

"Of course, but—"

"What were you thinking of when you erased that message?"

"I'm not even sure I did erase it."

The policeman looked at her for an endless few seconds before he asked, "Did your friend hear the message?"

Jennie hesitated before she answered. "No. I just told her about it."

"When did it come in?"

"Yesterday. In the evening."

"I mean the time. Your machine gives the time."

"I wasn't paying attention to that. I was trying to figure out the message."

"What time did you discover it?"

"It must have been eight. Eight-thirty. Sometime around there. Kate and I took the kids out for pizza. By the time we got home and I got them in bed—"

"Why didn't you report this immediately?"

"I called last night. Again this morning. But Sergeant Smith wasn't there."

"You could have left word."

"I tried. They told me he was at a hearing. Then they put me on hold. And forgot about me."

"Who'd you talk to?"

"I didn't get a name."

Somehow, without saying a word or changing expression, Goodley managed to give Jennie the impression he didn't believe her. He looked through the papers on his clipboard, and finally said, "That's all for now. Starting next week, I can reach you at Riverview Manor during the day. Right?"

"Not every day. It's part time. Three days a week."

"Oh?"

"Tuesday, Wednesday, and Thursday. Ten A.M. until two P.M."

He scribbled on the clipboard. "I'll be in touch." He turned to leave.

"There really was a message," Jennie said, and instantly wished she had not.

He spun on his heel and looked directly into her eyes. For the next half minute, the only sound in the room was the steady beat of his pen against his clipboard. He was standing a few feet from Jennie, close enough for her to be aware of the spicy, sharp scent of his aftershave.

Chapter Four

After talking to Jennie, Goodley went next door to get a statement from Kate.

She greeted him and led him down a short hall to the family room, where he paused briefly in the doorway, making a rapid analysis of the room he was about to enter.

White curtains, crisp and immaculate, covered the lower half of tall windows. A single book, easily recognizable as a cookbook, lay open on the coffee table. A few toys spilled from a stenciled wooden box near the fireplace but, overall, the space was as precise and tidy as the stars and stripes on a flag.

Kate's appearance was as all-American as her manner of decorating: slightly shorter than average and of a body type that, in a time of greater fashion tolerance, would have been described as "pleasantly plump." Short, curly hair framed a round, open face, with wide-set brown eyes and a small, upturned nose. A spattering of cinnamon freckles completed the apple-pie look.

"Would you like to sit down?" Kate offered, directing the policeman to the most comfortable-looking chair in the room.

He mumbled "Thanks," but eschewed the low recliner, selecting instead a no-nonsense Shaker bench, and began his questioning. "You were with Mrs. Connors at Barnstable's Flea Market yesterday. Correct?"

Kate nodded.

"Were you together the whole time?"

"Most of the time. I went off on my own for a little while."

"How long?"

"I don't know. Not long."

"Approximately?"

Kate thought about it a few minutes before answering. "Half an hour. Maybe forty-five minutes. No more than that."

"What did you do during that time?"

"I looked around the other tables. Mostly just browsed."

"And Mrs. Connors? Do you know how she spent that time?"

"Yes, that I do know. She was looking through boxes of records."

"How do you know this?"

"She told me. She met this old guy who sells records. An Englishman."

"Met him? You mean they had an appointment?"

"No. What I meant was, she met him while she was looking through the stuff on his table."

"Are you sure?"

"Yes."

Goodley asked, "How'd you get home from the police station?"

"Jennie's cousin picked us up. Didn't she tell you all this?"

Goodley said, "I'm just trying to reconstruct the day. Making sure I don't miss anything."

Kate nodded.

"Tell me about Mrs. Connors."

"What do you want to know?"

"What's she like?"

"A good friend. Generous. Do anything in the world for you. Fun to be around. Up for just about anything."

"Enemies?"

"I can't think of any. Well . . . you've seen Jen . . . sometimes when people first meet her they assume she's stuck up because of the way she looks. She's not."

"Would you say other women are jealous of her?"

Kate hesitated before she answered. "Probably."

"She's happily married?"

"Yes." There was no hesitation this time. "She's crazy about Tom, and vice versa. They met when she was a contestant for Miss Tennessee. It was love at first sight. A real fairy tale."

"What's he like?"

Kate thought a moment. "A good match for Jennie. They balance each other. He's serious. She's impulsive. He's older than she is."

"How much older?"

"Nine years."

Goodley was quiet a few minutes, looking over his notes. "Okay, tell me again how you and Mrs. Connors spent the day yesterday."

"We've already—"

"Just a general listing of your movements."

Kate sighed. "Well, we dropped the kids off at school. Since it was the first day, we had to get them settled, especially the two little ones. Trevor, that's my son, and Andy, he's Jennie's youngest, are both in first grade."

"Whose car did you drive?"

"Jennie's. We went to the flea market directly from school."

"What time was that?"

"We left for school at seven-thirty. It only takes about five minutes. We were in the building fifteen, maybe twenty minutes."

"Where was the car during this time?" Goodley asked.

"School parking lot."

"And before that?"

"Well, it was in their garage overnight."

"Do you know if they keep their garage locked?"

"Most of the time. Always when Tom's home. Jennie forgets sometimes."

Goodley was checking each point against his notes. "Go on," he said, looking up at Kate.

"I guess it was close to eight when we left school. Barney's is about a forty-five minute drive, so we must have gotten there around quarter to nine."

"Isn't that a long way just to buy records?"

"Jennie was looking for music to use in her work at the retirement community . . . you know . . . that age group. Somebody told her to try the flea market."

"Do you know who?"

"She didn't say. She just called one day last week and asked if I'd like to go along." Kate stopped to look at Goodley, who nodded for her to continue. "I said yes."

"Were there other tables with old records for sale?"

"I don't know. Probably. We zeroed in on this one because it was in the shade, and it was already getting hot. Anyway, he had a lot of stuff and, like I said, he and Jennie hit it off. Besides, he was really helpful."

"Unusually helpful?"

"What do you mean?"

"Did he help other customers too?"

"I guess so," Kate said. "I wasn't really paying that much attention. Actually, I'm just telling you what Jennie told me. They didn't start talking until after I'd left."

"When did you discover that the car was missing?"

"We were supposed to meet back at the car to get rid of our packages, and then have lunch. But when we went to put our stuff in the car, it was gone. You know the rest."

"What time was this?"

"Eleven-thirty. We wanted to hit the food pavilion before it got crowded."

Goodley looked at his notes. "It was twelve thirty-seven when you called the police station. An hour after you discovered the car was missing. What happened in that time?"

"We looked through the parking lot. Thought maybe we were wrong about where we parked."

Goodley interrupted, "Tell me about last night."

"There's not much to tell. Tom was out of town, and Frank, that's my husband, was working late, so we took the kids out for pizza."

"Whose idea was this?"

"Jennie's. She had a coupon. Said if I'd drive, she'd treat."

"What time did you get home?"

"About eight-thirty."

"When did you find out about the message on the answering machine?"

"This morning."

"Did you hear it yourself?"

"No. Jennie told me about it."

"Are you sure there was a message?"

"Why wouldn't I be?"

"When we listened to the tape just now, there was nothing about the car, nothing about Oz."

"Something happened to it then."

Goodley's look was noncommittal.

"If you'd seen Jennie this morning, you'd believe there was a message. Besides, I know she wouldn't lie. Jen's honest as the day is long."

"Why didn't you tell her to call the police?"

"I did. And, actually, she did call. Last night. Right after she got the message."

"How do you know this?"

"She told me so." There was a definite edge to Kate's voice.

Goodley either didn't notice or didn't care. He asked, "Weren't you worried this might be dangerous?"

"At first . . . but I didn't dream we'd really find the car. Jennie made it seem like such a lark to try. And when she gets an idea, she's hard to turn off."

"One more thing. The keys. Mrs. Connors said she hid them under the seat. Did she do this often?"

"Most of the time," Kate said. "She carries this humongous bag. Hates looking for things in it."

"Is it common knowledge she does this?"

"I don't know if I'd say common knowledge. People who know her well . . ." Kate hesitated, looking puzzled. "Sergeant Smith said some kids probably hot-wired the car. They didn't use the key."

"The vehicle was not hot-wired. It was started with a key the last time it was driven. And the key was put back under the seat."

Chapter Five

It was a little after nine. The kids were in bed, presumably asleep, as it was quiet in their room. Jennie sat at the kitchen table, with Kate hovering nearby.

"Just a few crackers," Kate urged.

"I'm fine."

"You're not fine."

Jennie's elbows were on the table, her face cradled in her hands, hair spilling over her shoulders in a dark, tangled mass. She looked at Kate, got up, went to the sink, and splashed cold water on her face. She set her shoulders and managed a weak smile when she rejoined Kate at the table and reached for a cracker. "Goodley give you a hard time?"

"Not too bad, actually. He mainly wanted to go over what we did yesterday. What time. Whereabouts of the car. Stuff like that. Here, have some cheese too. You haven't eaten since breakfast."

"You sound like my mother," Jennie said, but she accepted the cheese. That small bit of sustenance, together with Kate's matter-of-fact camaraderie, helped. "Speaking of my mother, I'd better call her. I'd hate for her and Daddy to read about this in the paper."

"Or see it on the news," Kate said.

"Oh, jeez, I didn't even think to watch the news tonight. Was it—"

"No. I watched while I was getting dinner and there wasn't anything yet. But you know it's just a matter of time." Kate lowered her voice, imitating the mellifluous tones of a TV newscaster, "The daughter of a distinguished naval chaplain murdered."

"What a mess. I wish—"

"It's not your fault, Jen. You're right about your parents, though. Better call them before Ellen does."

25

"I forgot about Ellen! She doesn't even know yet."

"She knows. She saw me in the yard with the kids and stopped to ask about the car. I told her."

"What'd she say?"

"She didn't say anything, but . . . well, you know Ellen."

"Don't start. She drove all the way up to Barney's to get us when we were stranded. Not everybody would do that."

"Right. And she made sure you were aware of that."

"She just likes to Mother Duck me. Always has."

"You don't let anyone else treat you like that."

Jennie waved off further discussion of Ellen. "That's the least of my worries right now. I don't think Goodley believes me about the tape."

"Yeah, he—"

"He what? What'd he say?"

"Not much. But he did mention it. Asked if I believed there was a message."

Jennie crumbled a cracker into bits. "Creep!"

"Anyway," Kate continued, "I told him yes, I was sure, and that something must have happened."

"You're absolutely right. Something did happen. I've got to find out what, because I'm positive . . . almost . . . I didn't erase the tape." When Kate started to interrupt, Jennie held up a silencing finger. "But somebody did. You know how you get vibes about your own space? When I came into the house with Goodley, I had the feeling something was wrong. And Smokey was acting really weird."

"For Smokey, that's normal."

"I'm serious."

"Too serious. You're driving yourself crazy."

Jennie looked into her friend's face and read the concern there. "Stop worrying. I'm not going to fall apart. Mainly, thanks to you. Giving the kids dinner . . ." She paused, remembering all that Kate had done in the past twelve hours, reached for her hand, and squeezed. "'Thanks' doesn't even begin to cover it." Tears filled her eyes, threatened to overflow.

"Cut it out. If you get sappy we'll both start crying."

"Probably," Jennie admitted, adding, "You look beat. You should be with Frank and the kids. Go on home."

Kate seemed ready to protest, but Jennie cut her off, and walked with her out to the driveway.

Alone after Kate went into the house next door, Jennie sat on the bench in her front garden. She usually enjoyed being outside after dark, loved the transforming magic of softened light on familiar objects, but this night held no magic. Sheet lightning revealed her neighbors' houses in outline, as though drawn with a black crayon. Then, lightning gone, the sky was dark, the houses swallowed by the massive blackness of the night. She went inside and locked the door against the dark shapes and the erratic sky. After calling her parents, she took a bath and went to bed with a magazine. Her hands turned pages while her mind went over the events of the past two days.

Two days? Incredible.

She got out of bed and wandered through the house, finally settling into her favorite chair, a Windsor rocker that had been in the family for generations, passed down to Jennie by her grandmother when Tommy was born. Smokey jumped into her lap. She stroked his head and ears as she looked idly around the room, a pleasant space filled with family pictures and comfortable, inviting furniture. Pieces of an antique spinning wheel hung over a brick fireplace; two walls were lined with bookshelves. She focused on the books, an eclectic assortment: the how-to books Tom collected, the romantic English fiction she loved, the children's books. An entire shelf was devoted to Frank Baum, remnants of her own childhood.

Whoever left that message knew me. Knew I'd be hooked if they mentioned Oz. She sat rigidly erect, stilling the natural motion of the rocking chair. *And whoever left the message erased it. Actually came into this house to get rid of the message they'd left. Who was it? And how did they get in?* She shuddered, startling the cat, who jumped down and scurried away.

She glanced at the clock when she saw the lights of the car turning into the driveway: 11:30. Guess the plane was late. Poor Tom. No idea what's in store for him. She had the door open before he could get his key in the lock. "Hi. Welcome home." She heard the false cheer in her greeting and wished she could start over.

"Where's the car?"

You could at least have kissed me before you asked. "It's a long story. Get comfortable and I'll make some coffee."

"You know I don't drink coffee this late." He stopped midway in the act of removing his already loosened tie, gave her a long look, and asked, "You okay?"

She tried to answer, could only nod.

"Have you had an accident?"

She shook her head.

"The kids?"

Still, no words would come.

He turned and ran down the hall to the boys' bedroom.

She saw a wash of light spill into the hall. *He wants to see their faces. Has to know they're safe.* She heard his footsteps crossing the floor to the space between their beds, imagined him bending over each child, brushing the hair back from each forehead. She loved him for that, and almost forgave him for not kissing her before asking about the car.

When he came back, she managed to get out, "They're okay. We're all okay."

And then he held her. Finally. Just held her. Tight against him until she could control the shaking. He stroked her hair and rocked her as a parent rocks a child. Even after she calmed down, she remained pressed against him, warmed by the heat of his body, lulled by the beating of his heart, choosing words to tell him. She tried to remember what she had told the kids, but could only remember their faces, the unusual quiet that hung in the air as they listened to her without interruption. She put her hand against Tom's chest and moved away from him.

"Better?" he asked.

She nodded and took another step back before she said, "I'm not sure it was true when I told you we're all okay. Something terrible has happened and we're involved." She paused. "It's complicated."

Telling him, she could not rid herself of the feeling of nightmare. No, nightmares go away when you tell them. This, she knew, would be a part of their lives forever—a major part for a while, gradually dimming, but never disappearing.

"Sure you don't want coffee?" she offered. "You won't sleep anyway."

In the kitchen, they stood side by side, arms touching, their eyes on the coffeemaker. "Gladys and Joe . . ." Jennie started, and then stopped, unable to find words to express what Robin's parents must be going through.

Tom remained silent.

More minutes passed, with only the gurgling of the coffeemaker to fill the void.

Jennie said, "Who are their friends? Are they really close to anyone?"

Still nothing from Tom.

"All those years in the navy. Moving around all the time. No real roots." *Why doesn't he say something?* "I guess they'll be okay. They've seen so much. His being a chaplain—"

"That won't help now. Not with this."

"No," she agreed, relieved to hear a voice other than her own.

At last the coffee was ready. She filled earthenware mugs and added sugar to hers.

Between sips, Tom began to speak. His voice was so low she heard only a few words of what he said, "Good people . . . shouldn't happen to them . . . their only child."

"He's kind of a bully though." *Had she really said that?*

"You mean Joe?"

"Um."

"Why do you think that?"

She shrugged, unwilling to say more, feeling guilty for criticizing at a time like this. However, the need to talk was strong and won out. "Nothing specific. I've just always had the impression that he ruled with an iron fist."

"Gladys seems happy."

"I meant Robin."

There was a long silence before Tom said, "Maybe she needed it."

"I don't think so. She was a nice kid. A free spirit, I guess, but last spring when she babysat so much, remember how attached Andy got?"

Tom stared into his coffee mug without answering.

Jennie watched him, and finally spoke again. "There's something else we need to talk about."

The mug lurched and coffee sloshed out over his hand.

"I can't even stand to say this." Five seconds—an eternity—passed. "I think . . ." She lifted her chin, defiant, and forced the words, "I'm pretty sure that lieutenant . . . Goodley's his name . . . I told you that, didn't I? Anyway, he thinks I did it. Killed Robin, I mean." The last words came in a rush.

Tom put his arms around her, drawing her to him. His chin rested on the top of her head so that his breath stirred her hair.

She moved closer to gather strength from his presence, but there was no respite there. His trembling matched her own. *He's tired,* she thought, *from that long trip. Coming home to this.*

Chapter Six

Goodley rang the doorbell, and then stepped back.

The man who opened the door was large, in both height and girth, and had a square, pleasant face, the kind that shows emotion clearly. This morning the emotion written there was grief.

Goodley nodded. "Morning, Mr. Langley."

Joe Langley stood aside and held the door open. Inside, he went to the foot of the stairs and called, "Gladys. The policeman's here."

"I'll be right down."

Almost immediately, a middle-aged woman, slight and finely drawn, came down the steps and joined them in the living room.

"Please sit down." Her gracious manner was at odds with her puffy eyes and the dark circles under them.

Goodley took a quick, appraising look around before he chose a chair directly in front of the window. A slant of morning sunlight outlined him, leaving his face in shadow, so that to the parents of the murdered girl, he was featureless, a silhouette in the shape of a man.

"Would you like a cup of coffee?" offered Mrs. Langley.

"No, thank you. I'm sure you want to get this over with as quickly as possible."

The Langleys seated themselves on the sofa on the other side of the room. The light that outlined Goodley was shining directly in their eyes, causing them to squint whenever they looked at him.

Joe went right to the point. "Do you have news for us?"

"Unfortunately, no. That's why I'm here. I need more information about your daughter."

"What else do you need to know?"

"Everything. The more I know about her, the better. Friends. School. Job. Hobbies. Anything you can think of."

"She was eighteen," began Gladys.

Joe interrupted, "We gave you all the information last night at the police station."

"I know, but I'd like to go over everything again. You've had a little more time and I thought you might remember something else." Goodley hesitated, studying each of their faces before he went on. "I know this is hard for you. But we can't afford to let too much time go by."

Gladys said, "Robin graduated from Christian Academy High School last spring." She seemed to gain strength as she spoke of her daughter.

Joe interrupted again. "That was in the paper."

"I'd rather get my information directly from you."

"I can understand that," Gladys said. "Robin would be starting college just about now. She planned to be a teacher. She was wonderful with children."

"Good student?"

There was the slightest tic of hesitation before Gladys answered. "She was an unusual girl. Very bright. Her teachers always remarked on that."

"An honor student?"

"Well, no. She was . . . a daydreamer. An artist really. Covered all her papers with—"

"He doesn't care about that," Joe said.

Goodley nodded at Gladys. "The more I know about your daughter, the better."

"Joe's right. It's nothing, really. She covered all her papers, all her book covers, with little drawings."

Goodley waited for her to add more. When she did not, he asked, "Did this create a problem in school?"

"Oh, no. Nothing like that."

Gladys was answering all the questions, more composed than her husband, though occasionally her voice seemed on the edge of breaking. Joe fidgeted, looked as though he wanted to interrupt, but did not. Finally, still without speaking, he got up and moved from the couch to a tall wing chair at the far end of the room. He moved with a prowling, animal grace. Away from his wife's presence, he seemed more agitated than ever.

"You said your daughter was enrolled in college?"

"Yes. University of Mississippi." Again, it was Gladys who answered.

Goodley looked up from his notes. "Active social life?"

Joe stared past Goodley, out the window. Gladys seemed to be studying the labyrinthine pattern in the carpet. When she looked up there were tears in her eyes. "To tell the truth, we didn't know very much about her social life the last two years."

"Two years?"

"That's when we moved here," Joe said.

Gladys twisted the tissue in her hands and whispered. "She got her driver's license a couple of months after that. And it was harder to keep track of where she was, who she was with."

Goodley's pen hovered over his clipboard. "Any indication of problems?"

"Not really," Gladys said, "at least not until about three, maybe four, months ago."

"What happened then?"

"There wasn't anything I could put my finger on, but I had the feeling something was bothering her."

"Did you ask what it was?"

"Yes. She insisted everything was fine."

"Did you believe her?"

"No, but I thought she would tell me in her own time if I didn't push. That had been my experience in the past. Now . . ." Gladys was unable to finish.

Goodley waited, allowing her to regain control before he prompted, "You say this was three or four months ago?"

"It was late spring," she finally said. "Not too long before graduation."

Goodley looked at Joe. "How about you? Any idea what was troubling your daughter?"

Joe shook his head.

"Boyfriend?" Goodley asked.

"Web Barrons. That's Webster James Barrons," Joe said.

Goodley made a note on the clipboard.

Joe continued, "A fine young man. Also enrolled at the University of Mississippi."

Goodley waited while Joe moved back to his former place beside his wife on the couch. "Last night at the police station, you said something about another young man."

"Brad Wilson." The father hissed the name.

Gladys put trembling fingers on her husband's arm.

Joe shook the hand off. "He killed her!" The words seemed to burst from him.

"You don't know that!"

"I know he's riffraff!"

"Why riffraff?" Goodley asked.

"Wait'll you see him." Joe turned to Gladys. "What do you call someone who goes around looking like that?"

Goodley sat perfectly still, his pen poised. He looked from Joe to Gladys, back to Joe. When neither of them spoke, he asked, "This Brad Wilson? Is he in school too?"

"No, he's older. Twenty-six, I think." Gladys' brow furrowed. "Yes, I'm sure that's what Robin said."

"Too old for her!"

Goodley waited for Gladys to respond to her husband's comment. When she did not, he asked, "Does he have a job?"

Joe answered, "He calls himself a musician. Plays guitar and sings. Loud, obscene garbage! That's what his kind calls music."

"You don't know that. You've never heard him play," Gladys said.

"He plays in a bar. Depends on drunks for his living." Joe stood up and began to pace.

"His relationship to your daughter?" prompted Goodley.

"None!" thundered Joe, coming to a stop in front of Goodley's chair.

"She loved him," Gladys said.

Joe moved again to the far end of the room, where he stood with his back to the others, his head bowed.

"Did he love her?" Goodley asked.

"I don't know," Gladys whispered. "I know she believed he did."

"And you think he killed her?" Goodley directed this question to Joe, who had turned around and was looking intently at Gladys.

"It's his fault she's dead."

"What do you mean?"

"I mean she's dead because of him."

"Because of him." Goodley repeated Joe's words. "In what way?"

"I don't know. But I know there's a connection. Because of him," Joe said, not taking his eyes from his wife's face, "our daughter is dead."

Gladys sat quietly, meeting his gaze, shaking her head, negating his statement.

Goodley watched them for a minute before he asked, "How did she meet him?"

"We don't know. He just started showing up," Joe said. "I put a stop to that. Forbid her to see him."

"She agreed?"

"She had no choice."

"So, she was no longer seeing him at the time of her death?"

Joe stood rigid, like a mechanical toy that's been robbed of its batteries.

"She was still seeing him," Gladys said softly. "She came to me. Asked me to try to reason with her father."

"And you agreed to help her sneak around behind my back!"

"She didn't want to sneak around. That's why she asked me to talk to you." Gladys touched a tissue to the corners of her reddened eyes.

Joe swallowed repeatedly. Neither spoke.

Goodley broke the silence. "How about the other young man? The Barrons fellow?"

Joe answered this time. "They went to school together."

"To the Christian Academy?"

"That's right."

"You approved of him?"

"He's from a good family."

"Your families are close?"

"I know his mother well. She's on the board of the retirement community where I work," Joe said. "Very active in the community. The Barrons family gives a great deal of time and money to worthwhile causes."

Goodley nodded as he wrote on his clipboard.

"Do you know how they felt about your daughter?"

"Oh, they liked her very much." Gladys spoke now. "In fact, Leda encouraged the relationship."

"Leda?

Gladys explained, "That's Mrs. Barrons, Web's mother."

"Could you describe how she encouraged the relationship?"

"Well, right after we moved in, Joe had just begun his chaplaincy at the hospital, and Leda gave a picnic to introduce us to people in the community. As soon as she saw Robin, she just seemed to take a liking to her. She was always inviting her to their home. I believe she thought Robin was good for Web. He's a bit of a rebel."

"Rebel?"

"Nothing serious," Joe said. "Just a few wild oats. Like young people do. I believe, though, that he is basically a fine young man. Otherwise, I would not have allowed my daughter to see him."

Goodley studied Joe a few seconds before he asked, "Any other friends she's especially close to? Anyone she might have confided in?"

"I don't know who it would be. No. I can't think of anyone." Gladys lowered her head and twisted the damp tissue. "We've moved around a lot, Joe being in the Navy, so Robin never had a chance to make close friends."

Goodley nodded, but made no comment.

A silence built in the room, which Gladys finally broke. "There's an address book on her bedside table."

"I'd like to see it."

"Of course."

While they waited for Gladys to return, Goodley turned to Joe. "This retirement community where you work, is it the one where Mrs. Connors is about to start work?"

"Yes, Riverview Manor. As a matter of fact, I suggested to the management that they offer Jennie the job as Activities Director. She's been volunteering with us for several years and is very good with the elderly. Quite talented musically, and, of course, pretty. People respond to that."

Gladys returned with a small paisley-covered book which she

handed to the lieutenant. "You'll return it when you're finished, won't you?"

"I'll take good care of it for you." He flipped through the pages before he dropped it into his pocket. Then he said, "About Mrs. Connors. Any idea why your daughter was found in her car?"

"No." Both of them answered at once.

"Any special connection to that family?"

"Only that she babysat for them."

"Did she babysit for other people too?"

"Yes, some. But mostly for the Connors. She gave swimming lessons to their little boys last summer and they were very fond of her."

"When was the last time she babysat for them?"

"I can't give you an exact date," Gladys said after a short pause. "It was at least a month, maybe several months ago. Robin didn't do much babysitting this past summer. She was busy with other things, getting ready for college and all. I think Jennifer called a couple of times, but Robin—"

"What difference does all this make, Lieutenant?" Joe asked.

"Maybe none. I'm trying to find some kind of pattern."

"Then you still have no idea who did this?"

"Let's just say there are a lot of pieces waiting to be put together."

"The other policeman told us that you were dusting the car for fingerprints. Did you find any?"

Goodley shook his head. "The car's clean. Someone was extremely thorough."

"How about the murder weapon. Have you found that?"

Goodley shook his head. "Like we told you, she was killed by a blow to the head with a heavy, probably metal, instrument."

"But you don't know what it was?"

"Not yet. Could have been a jack handle. The jack's missing from the Connorses' car."

"Stop fooling around and arrest that kinky-haired weirdo." The father's voice was something between a growl and a moan.

"You mean Brad Wilson?"

"You know who I mean!"

Chapter Seven

Y ou're not going to do anything foolish?"

"Of course not." Jennie answered Ellen's question and stood rigid when her cousin reached out to brush a tendril of hair from her face. *She still treats me like I'm six years old.*

"I'd be glad to drive you. If . . ." Ellen's voice trailed off.

"You don't have to take care of me." Jennie struggled to keep her tone even. *Be calm. How many people would loan you their car, anyway? She has a right to know what I plan to do with it.* "I have some errands. And I'd like to do them myself. I need to get back to normal."

When Ellen finally handed over the keys, Jennie thanked her profusely, made a beeline for the car, and then headed north toward River County.

She could not rid herself of the idea that the use of her vehicle as a hiding place for Robin's body had been a deliberate choice. So had the field that could be reached only by passing the small farmhouse with the flowers. "Left at Oz," the voice on the tape had said—and Jennie was hooked. That was not, could not, be random.

Seeking a respite from the endless questions, she turned on the radio, but the music, if anything, made it worse. One question, the most puzzling of all, throbbed through the beat of every song: *What common enemy do Robin and I have?* "You deserve. Her too." That's what the voice had said. *That must mean . . . What?*

When she passed the farmhouse, she looked for the woman among the flowers. Today she was nowhere in sight. Oz looked deserted. She turned at the crossroad. Almost there. She increased the volume on the radio and sang along, attempting to ease the tension.

Just before the road curved, she saw the small building. A pair of faded jeans hung from a line stretched between two trees. *Kate was right. Someone lives there.* She considered stopping to ask if they'd seen the maroon Taurus pass two days ago. *Maybe on the way home. Right now I have to go back to that field.*

She parked at the base of the ancient oak, in the same spot she and Kate had on the day they'd discovered Robin's body. When she locked Ellen's Toyota, the old adage about barn doors popped into her head, prompting a grim smile. A crow on a low-hanging branch screeched a warning. She ignored him and once again proceeded down the weedy gravel track on foot.

The car was gone now. The space where it had been was marked with yellow plastic ribbon. Heavy black letters proclaimed CRIME SCENE—KEEP OUT interminably along its sagging length. She hesitated only a few seconds before ducking under the tape and going directly to the area where the car had stood.

From there, she saw that the old road continued into the meadow and disappeared behind a barn that looked ready to collapse. The delapidated building stood on the crest of a small knoll, making it impossible to see how much farther the road extended or where it went. Grass and weeds stood semi-upright between narrow tracks leading from where the car had been to an area near the barn. Something about this bothered her. She studied the road in both directions, until, finally, it hit her: *The way the stalks are bent. It looks like they drove in from the other side.* She remembered the stiff, unbroken weeds scratching her bare legs as she walked toward the car two days ago and was convinced that was what had happened. *So they didn't pass by Oz. But they knew about Oz and used it to draw me here.* The thought fed her growing conviction that the terrible event had been directed at her as well as Robin, and was almost enough to make her turn back. She pushed it away, took a long, slow breath, and faced the crime scene.

Inside the cordoned-off area the vegetation was trampled, not quite uniformly. The tire marks of Jennie's car were easily discernible. Just beside them was a similar set of marks. *Maybe they drove the police van out here.* She considered this briefly, and then shook her head. *The way the weeds are broken down . . . these tire marks* were made by someone coming from the barn. Besides, I was with the police, and I know how careful they were not to disturb the area. There were two narrow lines cutting across the space between the two sets of tracks. The killer must have dragged Robin's body between the two cars. She shivered and tried to banish that image.

Remembering Goodley's actions of the previous day, she made the same slow rotation, using her hands as a shield against the sun's glare. The meadow contained nothing that seemed to her unusual, and she couldn't see more than a few feet into the thick woods that bordered the field on two sides. As she completed her circle, she saw someone standing at the treeline on one side. She tensed, wondering how long the shadowy figure had been there. Towering pines dwarfed the human form so that she could not judge the height or even be certain of the gender of the figure, though she would have described it as male, not particularly tall.

The figure stepped back into the shade.

Jennie remained where she was, considering that her scrutiny might antagonize him, but afraid to look away.

The figure stooped and lifted something from the ground.

What's he doing? The object was long and slender. A walking stick? That seemed the right size and shape. A rifle? She realized it was the right size and shape for that too, and she started back toward the car. Sounds of snapping twigs from the woods told her that the enigmatic figure was following along with her, staying just within the treeline. She moved quickly, but did not allow herself to run. When she came to the spot where the small lane entered the wooded area, the sounds stopped. Keeping her steady pace, she wondered why. Was it just her presence at the crime scene that had upset him? Was he taking aim with the rifle? She had by now convinced herself that it was indeed a rifle. Abandoning even the appearance of calm, she began to run.

She was almost to the spot where she had left Ellen's car when she saw a gray Jetta parked in the road beside the borrowed vehicle. A tall figure stood between the two cars. She saw only his back, but he appeared to be writing down a license number. Goodley! Jennie stopped so abruptly that she slipped on the loose gravel and fell to her knees.

He spun around. "What're you doing here?"

She picked herself up and answered with as much dignity as she could muster, "I just wanted to look around. See if I could figure out what happened."

"Leave that to me."

But she had to know if she'd been right about the direction of the vehicle. "Did you drive the police van down to the meadow?"

Goodley said nothing.

She interpreted his silence as a warning, but persisted. "Did you?"

"Tampering with a crime scene is a serious offense."

"I didn't tamper with anything. I was just looking around."

He studied her with his usual infuriating lack of expression. "I'll do the looking. You stay away from here. I'm telling you that for your own good."

When she opened her mouth again, Goodley shook his head.

Common sense told her to back off and, for once, she listened. She smiled and made the lip-zipping motion she used with the kids, a universal signal of promised quiet.

He almost smiled back, or so she thought. With a face like Goodley's, it was hard to tell. He got into the Jetta, backed up, giving her space to pull easily into the road, and motioned for her to leave.

Keeping her promise of silence, she drove away, wondering if the figure in the woods had seen Goodley. Was that why he stopped? She was pretty sure the police lieutenant had not been aware of the other person. *I should have told him,* she thought, and considered going back. *No. My best bet is to keep out of his way.*

Driving home, she alternated between thinking about the figure in the trees—Who was he? What was he doing there?—and wondering why Goodley had not demanded more explanation of her presence. More to the point, was it a good or a bad sign that he had not?

Chapter Eight

FUNERAL OF GIRL FOUND DEAD
IN BEAUTY QUEEN'S CAR

Jennie stared at the headline and fumed. "As if things aren't bad enough."

Tom came into the kitchen and stood at her shoulder, squinting down at the words on the page.

"I am not a beauty queen."

"First runner-up," he pointed out. "That's close." He put his hand on her arm, added, "If I'd been—"

"For heaven's sake, stop! That was over ten years ago. What does it have to do with"—she gave the newspaper an angry snap—"anything?" She lowered the page so she could look at him. "You're in here, too." She read: *"Former University of Tennessee track star, presently employed by Southern Automated Information Systems, Inc. as a software development specialist."*

Tom groaned. "SAIS will love that. What else does it say?"

"Here. Read it yourself." She handed the paper across the table to him.

He read aloud: *". . . 18-year-old daughter of retired navy chaplain, presently a chaplain at Military Hospital of the South, also serves as visiting clergy to local retirement community, decorated war hero . . .* Did you know that?"

"What?"

"That Joe was a decorated war hero?"

"It doesn't surprise me. He has that quality about him."

"What quality?"

"You know. Uncompromising."

Tom continued to read.

She looked out the window, and then at the clock. "Almost time to go. Think I should call Mom and check on the kids before we leave?"

"I'm sure she has everything under control."

"Control," she repeated after him, and buried her face in her hands.

He put a hand on her shoulder. "We don't have to go. Everyone will understand. Frankly, I'd just as soon . . ."

The warmth of his hand and the pressure of his fingers felt good. She took her hands from her face and stood up. "So would I, but we do have to go."

When they arrived at the church, a van with the familiar blue and yellow logo of a local television station was parked across the street. Jennie held on tightly to Tom's arm with one hand and with the other brushed the hair from her face. Her skirt was blowing, lashing against the back of her knees. Miniature tornado-shaped spirals of dust rose from the gravel in the parking lot. "I hope the rain holds off," she said.

Tom looked doubtfully at the sky.

When they reached the sidewalk leading from the parking lot to the front door, someone stuck a microphone in Jennie's face.

"You're the one who found the body, aren't you?"

Jennie looked past the microphone to the perfectly groomed young woman with eyes as round and blank as the glass button eyes of a teddy bear. Behind her was another figure, with long, blue-jeaned legs. The face and torso above the legs were partially obscured by a camera lens.

Tom turned sideways, so that his body formed an ineffective shield for Jennie. "Please. She has nothing to say."

The woman persisted, skipping around him to Jennie's other side, teddy bear eyes glittering. "Would you care to comment?"

Tom interrupted, less polite this time, "Leave her alone."

Jennie gripped his hand tighter. He was shaking too. Somehow they made it into the church, past the strange faces and the equipment. Sergeant Smith was just inside the door. He smiled at Jennie as she passed. Goodley stood as though at attention against the back wall of the sanctuary, less obvious because he didn't wear a uniform. No smile from him.

Tom distracted her with a whisper. "There's Ellen. She's alone. Shall we sit with her?"

Jennie nodded.

Joe and Gladys Langley were seated in the front pew, close together, arms touching, backs straight. *I'm glad I can't see their faces,* Jennie thought. *That's Web Barrons sitting with them. Odd.* She looked around for Brad Wilson. *Where is he? I thought Robin and Brad . . .* She tried to remember what Robin had said. Maybe he's sitting farther back. She wanted to turn around and look, decided she should not. She concentrated on the front rows, scanning: Joe and Gladys. Two frail-looking elderly people. Probably Robin's grandparents. Web. His parents. A lot of young people, some of whom she recognized as members of last year's Academy football team.

The service droned on. She looked again at Joe and Gladys. Their rigid stillness, their squared shoulders, struck her as more tragic than if they had been collapsed in tears.

She tried to follow the words of the minister, but couldn't force herself to concentrate. The music started. She felt Tom's hand on her elbow and stood with the rest of the congregation. The solemn tones of the organ and a few words came through, familiar words that she had sung many times without considering their meaning: "*. . . the darkness deepens . . . change and decay in all around I see . . . oh, Lord, abide with me.*"

She reached for Tom's hand and held it tightly, glad of his presence, the reassuring animal warmth of him beside her. More words— something about earth's vain shadows. Frightening words, made less frightening by the blending of human voices. The familiar sounds settled her a little. She looked toward the window, mercifully not a stained glass picture, but a real window. There were dogwoods planted along the side of the church, and it was from these trees, from the bold, sure pattern of their deeply veined leaves and the promise of their swollen tips that she at last drew some peace. The threatened rain was beginning to fall.

Finally the service ended. The minister closed his Bible. The organ was silent. Joe and Gladys followed their daughter's casket down the aisle. Still in her place beside Tom, Jennie watched as they and the other mourners filed out. Most were people she knew, many she recognized as friends of Robin, kids she was used to seeing in jeans and T-shirts. They seemed out of place in the dress-up clothes they wore today. Their smooth, young faces were uneasy. There was none of the jostling, the purposeful, pseudo-accidental bumping into one another's bodies that was usually so much a part of their movement.

Goodley caught Jennie's eye and squinted an indecipherable message. Oblivious to good manners, he elbowed his way through the crowd until he was beside her and Tom.

"Follow me," he said.

Without question, Tom did as he was told, and Jennie, with his hand firmly on her arm, had no choice but to go along. Goodley led them through the pastor's study and out the side door. She saw that he was helping them avoid the young reporter and her cameraman, whose attentions were focused on the front door.

"Thanks," she said, and was going to add more when she became aware of the quiet, unnatural in such a large crowd. Everyone was turned toward the street. There was Brad Wilson, scruffy in cutoff Levi's and a torn shirt. Some memory danced just beyond her reach. Then the young man moved, just a slight shift of torso, but it was enough to jog her memory, and she knew he was the shadowy figure who had watched her from the treeline a few days ago. What was he doing there? She wondered briefly if he'd been following her. *Don't be silly. It has nothing to do with you. He loved Robin.* The look on his face now, even seen from a distance, left no doubt about that. *He'd want to see where her body was found. But he didn't come to the service. That's strange.*

She studied him and tried to remember what Robin had told her about their relationship. He looked desperate, almost feral. His beard and his curly, reddish-blond hair, loose from its usual ponytail, formed a shifting, incongruous halo around an angular face. He seemed oblivious to the wind and the light rain pelting him as he leaned against his van, staring at the front of the church. Jennie looked to the place where his eyes were directed and saw Web Barrons standing with Robin's parents at the circular driveway in front of the church. The three of them had stopped, and both Joe and Web were returning Brad's stare. Gladys tugged at her husband's arm, saying something that Jennie could not hear. Finally, Joe responded and the two of them got into the waiting limousine.

The driver started the engine and its low growl woke up the crowd, including the newspeople. The blue-jeaned man ran toward the street, holding his camera aloft as if it were a banner. The reporter minced after him as fast as her too-tight skirt would allow. Brad scrambled into the van and slammed the door shut. A grinding sound issued from under the hood. Then silence. His head moved skyward and his lips formed the familiar four-letter word as the news crew crossed the twenty-five feet of lawn between the arc of the drive and the street. Brad rolled up his window and almost trapped the offending microphone. Again the grinding sound. And again silence. When the engine finally caught, the crowd let out its breath collectively. The reporter just managed to jump out of the way as the van lurched into motion.

Chapter Nine

Goodley eased his car onto the high ground between the deep ruts of the short driveway and set the hand brake. He leaned back in the seat, studying the surrounding area, postponing the moment when he must leave the comfort of the air-conditioned vehicle.

The house, its unpainted sides polished silver by the elements, was positioned a few feet to the right of the driveway. A plank door stood partially open. There were two small windows, set high in the wall. Through them Goodley could see white, ruffled curtains. In one of the windows a plant pushed against the screen. Geraniums grew along the front of a crude porch fashioned from huge logs cut in half and set in a mound of dirt. Half a dozen tomato plants filled a small spaded-up area beside a strip of coarse gravel. To the left of the driveway was a clearing, about fifty feet wide. Trees came to within a few yards of the house in back and, looking over the roof, Goodley judged that they grew even closer on the side hidden from him.

A van rested at the end of the drive in the shade of a massive oak. He recognized it as the vehicle that had been parked in front of the church the day of the funeral. Hanging from the nearly parallel limbs of the tree were a number of birdhouses. Some were fashioned from hollowed-out gourds, others from mismatched bits of unfinished wood. The birds seemed to appreciate the odd assortment. The area was alive with darting activity.

In the short time it took Goodley to register these details, the front door had opened further. When he stepped from his car, a young man, slightly built and of medium height, came onto the porch. He was dressed in jeans, wearing neither a shirt nor shoes, and had long, reddish-blond hair pulled back into a ponytail.

"Help you?" he asked.

Goodley flashed the badge in the leather wallet. "Lieutenant Weston Goodley."

"I know who you are. Been expecting you."

Caught off guard, Goodley nodded. The two men studied each other with open curiosity for a few seconds before the younger one said, "And you know I'm Brad Wilson."

"Yes," Goodley answered. "I guess you know why I'm here."

"Yeah."

"Let's get started then. What can you tell me about Robin Langley?"

"You wanna come in? Get out of the sun?"

"That would be nice."

The house was one large room, sparsely furnished. Shelves were attached to the back wall on either side of a door that stood open. The shelves were filled with books, mostly paperbacks with scarred covers, records, and stereo equipment. An acoustic guitar hung from a hook in the wall. An oscillating fan, positioned in the center of the room between the two doors, made wide sweeps, stirring the air.

"Want a beer?" Brad asked, opening the refrigerator.

Goodley shook his head.

"Don't drink on duty, huh?"

"No."

"Mind if I have one?" Without waiting for an answer, he took a bottle of Miller's Draft from the old-fashioned, round-topped refrigerator, opened it, and took a long swig before he turned back to Goodley. "Have a seat."

Goodley looked around, and then sat in the chair indicated by Brad's outstretched arm, a cane-bottomed rocker with a stack of books next to it. He read the title of the top volume, *Mexico City Blues* by Jack Kerouac, and noticed that there were bits of paper stuck in various places. He waited a moment for Brad to sit down. When he did not, Goodley leaned back so that the rocking chair was poised at the back edge of its rockers.

"Tell me about your relationship with Miss Langley."

"What do you want to know?"

"Let's start at the beginning. How did you meet her?"

"Southern Lites. You know the place?"

Goodley nodded. "Heard of it. Supposed to have the best catfish platter in the county."

"You got it. Anyway, I work there. Play guitar. Sing. Robin came in one night with some other kids."

"When was this?"

"Weekend before Easter."

"Easter this year?"

"Yeah."

Goodley did a quick calculation. "That would be five, almost six months ago."

Brad nodded.

"Wasn't she a little young for that place?"

Brad was still on his feet, prowling from one side of the room to the other while he talked. He paused to take one of the chairs tilted against a wooden table in the corner and placed it so that the oscillating fan just touched him on the far edge of its sweep before he answered.

"They all were. Too young, that is. They had phony IDs that didn't fool anybody. Zac got rid of them. You know Zac? Zachary McHugh? He owns Southern Lites."

"I know his reputation."

"Well, it's true. He runs a clean place. It's not for kids, but it's clean."

"So he got rid of the kids. How'd you get to know Miss Langley?"

"The others, the other four—there were six in all—they left with no argument when Zac asked them to—" Brad stopped, shook his head. "Not the Barrons brat."

"You mean Webster Barrons?"

"Yeah."

"That's who Miss Langley was with?"

"Right. The other four were together in one car. Robin and Web came in his little red sports number. He'd obviously been drinking already and he tried to talk Zac into selling him another six-pack."

"Where'd all this take place?"

"Just inside the door. The bar area."

"And where were you?"

"On stage. The ruckus started during my set. When the set ended, I came over to the bar for a beer. I was watching this kid, turned out to be Barrons, give Zac a hard time . . . I almost bumped into Robin. She was just standing there, looking around. Seemed kind of lost. Out of place. She asked me where the ladies' room was and I told her. She was so small, at first I thought she was a little kid." His voice broke on the last few words.

Goodley gave him a little time before he prompted, "Go on."

"So, anyway, by the time Robin came back from the ladies' room, Zac had finally convinced Web that he wouldn't sell him any beer, and the kid was pretty mad, but he was ready to leave. Robin told him she thought she should drive. Well, that sent him over the edge. He said he was sick of everybody telling him what to do. It was clear he wasn't going to give in. Let her drive. She looked scared. I offered to drive her home."

"She accepted? Just like that?"

"What's that supposed to mean?"

"Nothing special."

"Yeah, sure. Anyway, just for the record, she didn't accept right away. She asked if there was a phone she could use to call somebody. Zac said sure. Then she bought a Coke and we sat and talked until it was time for my next set. She decided to stick around and listen to a couple of songs. By this time she knew I wasn't just hittin' on her. I guess she knew she could trust me. She ended up staying until I was finished and, to make a long story short, I drove her home."

"And after that?"

"What do you mean?"

"Did you see her on a regular basis after that?"

"Yeah. The next week we had a date. I picked her up, rang the doorbell, met her folks, the whole bit. We started going out pretty regular. Then her old man decided he didn't like my looks. Told me to get lost."

"What did she do?"

"Well, he's a real military type. Nobody ever stood up to him. So she asked me to lay low for a while."

"And did you? Lay low?"

"Sort of."

"'Sort of'? What does that mean?"

"I kept out of sight of the old man. She met me at different places."
Brad stopped and gave Goodley a long, hard look. "She wasn't
sneaky. Don't think that. She told her mother about it, even asked
her to talk to the old man." Brad paused as the fan touched him with
its sweep, making a flutter of the curly hair on his chest and beard.
Savoring the moving air, he waited until the fan turned away before
he continued, "Funny thing is, the old man loves that Barrons kid,
thinks he's a great guy, but he's real trouble."

"Trouble? In what way?"

"All ways. Drinks like a fish. Terrible temper. That's why he was
in private school. He'd been kicked out of two high schools before
he went to the Academy. He was always getting into fights. But his
parents had money and they covered for him. They gave him that
car. Gave it to him. The little punk's never had to work for anything
in his life." Brad got up from the chair and went to stand in front of
Goodley. "You talked to him?"

"Not yet."

"Yeah, well, when you do, don't believe everything you hear. He
couldn't take it when Robin dumped him."

"What're you saying?"

"Just take anything he says with a grain of salt."

"I'll keep that in mind."

Brad tipped the bottle approvingly toward Goodley and went
back to his chair.

Goodley watched him closely as he asked, "What was your relationship with Miss Langley at the time of her death?"

"We were gonna get married."

Goodley rocked gently. "Married?"

"Married." Brad repeated the word slowly, and combed his beard
with his fingers before he continued. "It was all worked out. Before
school started. Robin didn't want to go to college. At least not yet.
She didn't know what she wanted to do, but she knew she didn't
want to be a teacher. That was her old man's idea."

"Did her mother know about this? That you were getting married?"

"No. We were gonna just do it. Drive down to New Orleans and get married. It was all planned. A neighbor, Mrs. Deighton, was going to cover for us for a few days."

"Mrs. Deighton?" Goodley repeated the name. "You mean Ellen Deighton? Mrs. Connors' cousin?"

"I don't know her first name. But, yeah, I think she's related to the Connorses somehow. She lives right around the corner from Robin. Same street the Connorses live on. Robin babysat for the Deightons' little girl sometimes."

"And this Mrs. Deighton was going to help you?"

"Yeah, I know. Now that I think about it, it's hard for me to believe too, but I didn't think about it at the time. I was too happy with the way things were working out. Now I can't help but wonder if maybe the old man found out."

"Oh?"

"That old buzzard hates my guts. He'd do anything to keep his daughter away from me."

"Even kill her?"

No answer from Brad.

"You haven't answered my question."

"I don't know the answer to your question. He's a fanatic. I don't know what he'd do."

"That why you didn't come into the church for the funeral?"

"You got it."

Goodley watched the young man for a few minutes before he stood up. "One more question: Any idea why the girl ended up in the Connorses' car?"

Brad gave Goodley a long, hard look, and then stared at the floor a few seconds before he answered. "No."

"You're sure?"

"Yeah."

"You look like . . ."

"Like what?"

"Like maybe you have something you want to say."

Brad shook his head.

Goodley waited, watching, before he asked, "How well do you know the Connorses?"

"I picked Robin up at their house a couple of times after babysitting and she talked about them some."

"What'd she say?"

"Nothing special. They were . . ." Brad stood up, went to the door, and looked out before he added, "Who knows? Who knows about anybody?"

Chapter Ten

Goodley removed the badge from his jacket while he waited for someone to answer the doorbell. The woman who responded was tall and strikingly attractive.

"Mrs. Deighton?"

"Yes, I'm Ellen Deighton."

Goodley held up the badge. "Lieutenant Weston Goodley."

"I know. I saw you at Robin Langley's funeral. I was with my cousin."

"I'd like to ask you some questions in connection with the death of Miss Langley."

"Certainly. Come in."

He took a moment to savor the cool air that flowed around him when he stepped across the threshold onto the gleaming marble tile of the foyer. "Nice in here," he said, "especially on a day like this."

Ellen led the way into the living room.

Goodley sat down in a chair too low for his long legs.

"Would you excuse me a moment," she said. "I left a glass of iced tea in the kitchen. Do you mind if I get it?"

"No."

"Could I get something for you?"

"Nothing for me."

While she was gone, he admired the watercolor above the sofa, a tranquil view of English countryside. Scanning the room, he noted that everything about it was restful. Pale fabrics covered the sofa and chairs. A crystal bowl glittered on an end table. Tiny wildflowers, intricately embroidered on white pillows, provided the only bright hues. Dark woods, polished to a soft glow, contrasted with the icy pallor of the other surfaces. He continued to look around the room, seeking a clue to its mistress, a hint that would divulge some secret of personality. But he found only a cool perfection—nothing to belie his first impression. No clutter. Not even a dusty corner. A well-organized household. Even the meticulously embroidered pillows were carefully arranged. He was pondering this when Ellen came back into the room.

"Such a shame about Robin," she said. "The whole neighborhood's in shock. I hope you find whoever did this." She sat on the sofa, rearranging the pillows as she spoke. "But I'm not sure how I can help you."

"I never know myself what's going to be helpful. Just tell me what you know about Miss Langley."

"Well, I attend the same church as the Langleys. So I knew Robin from there. Also the Swim Club. She'd been a lifeguard for the past two summers. I'm the club secretary, so I write the checks, including paychecks. I had some contact with her there. My daughter, Elizabeth, was in the beginner's swimming class that Robin taught. And occasionally, actually only a few times, she babysat for Elizabeth." Ellen stopped. She stirred the cubes in the tea with her finger. "Really, I don't know what you're looking for."

"Neither do I. Anything to get a clearer picture of the girl's life. Something in it led to her death."

"Of course. But, to me, she was just a sweet child, an innocent really."

Goodley studied her carefully before he said, "I'd like you to be direct with me. So I'll be direct with you. Did you plan to help Robin Langley elope with Brad Wilson?"

Ellen set her drink on the table and took her time answering. "Why do you think that?"

"Did you?"

She didn't answer.

"Someone told me that they had plans to elope. Drive down to New Orleans and get married, and that you were going to help them. 'Cover for them for a few days' is how it was put to me."

Ellen sighed. "I had hoped Joe and Gladys would be spared this."

"So, it is true?"

"Well . . . yes and no."

"Would you explain that?"

"The truth is rather complicated."

No comment from Goodley. He sat with his pen poised over the clipboard.

"Robin talked to me about going to New Orleans to marry Brad. That's true. And she did ask if I would give her mother a letter . . . after enough time had elapsed so they would already be married by the time Gladys read it."

"And you agreed?"

"Well, I didn't actually agree. But, on the other hand, I didn't tell her no."

Goodley heard this with raised eyebrows.

Ellen explained, "I thought she was nervous about going to college and that this whole marriage business was just an escape. I hoped if she had someone to confide in, she'd get over her jitters. When the time came, she'd go to school. Once there, she'd adjust, and the whole thing with Brad would blow over." She paused, and, after a few seconds, added, "Actually, I think something close to that happened. A couple of weeks ago, she talked to me again. Said she was having second thoughts about the plan."

"Did she say why?"

"Only what I just told you."

"Did she tell you how Wilson felt about this?"

"No."

"And you didn't ask her?"

"She was terribly confused. Certainly not ready for marriage. But, you know how young people dig their heels in when you argue with them. I didn't want to say anything that would make her do that."

"Yet you would have assisted her in the elopement?"

"I told you. I thought by giving her a chance to talk, she would realize it wouldn't work. That the whole idea was just a fantasy."

"And you think that's what happened?"

She hesitated. "Well, something changed her mind."

"Could there have been someone else?"

"I wondered about that. If there was, she didn't tell me about him."

"Did you talk to her often?"

"Every day until the pool closed. Most of the time, it was just casual conversation. She didn't always talk about personal matters. And I never brought them up."

"When did the pool close?"

"The weekend before she died."

"Seems a little early to close a swimming pool. There's still another month of hot weather."

"We don't close completely. It's just a small community pool and once school starts, we're only open on weekends. Sometimes, if it's really hot, we open for an hour or so in the evening. Our regular lifeguards go back to college and several of us who have kept our lifesaving certificates current fill in. As I said, it's community-owned and pretty casual."

"Tell me how Miss Langley fits into this picture."

"The head lifeguard—Robin held that position this summer—makes sure all the keys are turned in, that sort of thing, and then meets with a member of the Board, and they have sort of a wrap-up session." She paused. "I was the person she was supposed to meet and return the keys to."

Goodley sat up straighter. "Supposed to meet?"

"The meeting was scheduled for Monday, but she failed to show up."

"This past Monday?"

"Yes."

"That's the day she was killed."

Ellen nodded.

"What happened?"

"I went to the pool. That's where we were scheduled to meet, but—"

"What time was this?"

"We were supposed to meet at eight."

"A.M. or P.M.?"

"A.M. Robin wanted to make it early because she had a lot to do that day, so I went there directly after taking Elizabeth to school."

"How long did you wait?"

"I don't really know. At least an hour. Maybe more."

"Did you attempt to call her?"

"No. The telephone in the clubhouse had already been disconnected. And my cell phone wasn't working."

"You didn't try to reach her from another phone?"

"No. I just assumed she forgot. I didn't think too much about it.
Figured she would remember later, call me to apologize, and we
could reschedule."

"This didn't upset you?"

"I was annoyed, but I told you . . . it's a community organization.
Almost like a family. One makes allowances."

"When did you hear she'd been killed?"

"I think it was the next day. Yes, Tuesday. Kate Britten told me. I
saw her in the yard and stopped to ask if Jennie'd heard anything
about the car. I was the one who drove up to River County to pick them
up when the car was missing." She hesitated, looked embarrassed.
"I suppose you already know that."

He nodded.

"Anyway, that was the first I knew about this dreadful thing."

"This is Saturday. Why haven't you talked to the police before?"

"I wasn't sure what I should do."

"You should have called us immediately. Any information about
that day could be vital."

"Yes, I can see that now. But before . . . this whole horrid mess . . .
someone in our neighborhood being murdered—"

Goodley tapped the clipboard with his pen. "I understand you're
related to the Connorses."

"Yes. Jennie and I are cousins."

"Close?"

"To Jennie, you mean? So-so. She's ten years younger. Actually,
I'm probably closer to Tom. He and I were friends in school."

"Friends? By that you mean . . ."

"I mean *friends*." There was acid in Ellen's voice.

"I have to check every possibility."

"As a matter of fact, I introduced Tom to Jennie." She leaned forward to bring the edge of a magazine into perfect alignment with
the side of the table as Goodley watched.

"You look very much like your cousin," he told her.

"People do say that we look alike."

"How close was your cousin to the murdered girl?"

"Haven't you talked to her about that?"

"I'm just trying to get another perspective."

"I see. Well, Tom and Jennie were much closer to Robin, to the whole Langley family, in fact, than I was. She babysat for them a lot. Last spring, my uncle, Jennie's father, had a heart attack, and Robin stayed with Tommy and Andy, day and night, for a week or more, so Jennie could be with her mother."

Goodley made a notation on the clipboard. "Anything else you can tell me about Robin Langley? How well did she get along with her coworkers at the Swim Club?"

"No conflicts that I knew of."

"The young fellow who sat with the family at the funeral, Webster Barrons? Did you know him?"

"I know who he is. The Barronses don't belong to the club. They live over in The Oaks. Have their own pool. But Webster visited us several times as Robin's guest."

"Did he ever create a problem?"

"A shoving incident one time. I think maybe another boy was paying too much attention to Robin."

Chapter Eleven

Jennie watched Goodley hold the pieces of the muddy jack an arm's length away from his immaculate white shirt and sharply creased tan slacks. She restrained herself from answering the accusation she read in his compressed lips.

Tommy asked, "Is it the murder weapon?"

Goodley didn't answer.

"Wow!" Andy was bouncing in excitement. "We found the murder weapon."

On hearing her sons speculate on this grisly subject, Jennie couldn't keep quiet any longer. "He didn't say that."

"The guy on TV said Robin was killed with a heavy metal object." As usual, Tommy sounded older than his eight years.

Andy was practically doing a war dance now. "Wow," he repeated. "The cops couldn't find it. But me and my brother—we did."

When Goodley didn't respond to any of these comments, Jennie asked, "Do you think Robin Langley was killed with this?"

"I won't know until Forensics runs their tests. Maybe not even then." He placed the pieces in a heavy plastic bag. "Their job would be a lot easier if you hadn't let your kids play with it."

"I didn't let them play with it," she reminded him. "They found it in the creekbed and I called you immediately."

Without comment, Goodley slowly and methodically placed the bag in the car, and then directed his attention to the boys.

"Show me exactly where you found the jack." His usual formal manner softened and he reached out a hand to each child.

Jennie nodded to the boys and, taking her cue, they led her and

Goodley to the shallow creek that separated their yard from the woods behind.

"It was right here," Tommy said, coming to a halt by a large boulder a few yards beyond the edge of the Connorses' property.

Goodley squatted, hands on knees, and peered into the shallow depression in the soft earth next to the rock. After a few seconds, he looked over his shoulder toward the children. "Tell me exactly where the jack was."

Tommy moved closer, leaned over, and pointed to an area where the hole was deeper than the main depression and extended, tunnel-like, under the edge of the rock. "Right here, like it was . . ." The child paused and narrowed his eyes in concentration as he continued, "partly under the rock, and the part sticking up was almost covered with leaves and sticks."

"Was it in one piece? Or separated?"

"Separated. Just like now."

"How'd you happen to find them?" Goodley asked.

"We were looking for stuff to build our fort."

"You guys have a fort?"

"Not yet," Tommy admitted. "We're still getting the stuff together to build it."

Goodley prompted him, "And you thought the jack might fit in?"

"No." Tommy's tone was patient. "We were looking for old boards, things like that. And we just found—"

Andy broke in, "Yeah, we knew it was supposed to go together. To hold up the car when you fix a tire. So we took it to Mommy."

Jennie interrupted to remind Goodley, "That's when I called you."

"Is this from your car?"

She shrugged. "I don't know. Those things all look alike to me."

Goodley turned back to the boys. "You guys play here every day?"

They nodded at him. Tommy said, "Unless it rains. Then Mom won't let us 'cause it's too muddy."

"Did you play here yesterday?"

"No."

Jennie said, "It rained the day before and the ground hadn't dried out yet."

Goodley lifted one foot and checked the bottom of his shoe. "Still pretty soft. Drains fast, though, because of the gravel." He spoke softly, as though to himself, and continued to pace the area surrounding the boulder, going as far as the small creekbed.

Jennie noted the same concentrated energy she'd seen when he examined the car with Robin's body in it. She reached for her sons and put a hand on each of them, whether for their sake or hers, she could not have said.

Tommy asked, "Are you looking for footprints?"

Goodley nodded.

"See any?" Andy asked.

"Well, I see the prints of all our shoes."

Though his tone when he spoke to Jennie was brusque and faintly accusing, he answered the boys' questions with surprising patience.

The sound of a car drew their attention.

"There's Daddy."

The three Connorses turned to Goodley.

He answered their unspoken query. "Go ahead. I don't need you here right now. I'll probably stop in with a few more questions before I leave."

Andy ran toward the driveway, shouting, "Daddy, Daddy, guess what!"

But Tommy's longer legs covered the ground faster. "We found the murder weapon," he yelled.

Tom stopped midway in his reach into the car for his suit jacket and looked over the boys' heads toward Jennie.

She said, "I think maybe they did."

"What? How?"

"They were playing by the creekbed and they found a jack . . . you know, for a car, half-buried under that big rock."

"Did Goodley say it's the murder weapon?"

"Not in so many words, but he sure is interested. And right now he's back there checking for—"

Tom interrupted, "Is it from our car?"

She hunched her shoulders. "I don't know. He asked me that too."

Tom looked toward the policeman, who was now striding through their yard.

Goodley nodded a greeting as he came closer.

Tom said, "My boys tell me they found the murder weapon."

Without answering, Goodley went to his car and held up the bag containing the pieces of metal encrusted with mud and leaves. "This yours?"

Tom stepped closer and reached for the bag. "Mind if I take it out for a closer look?"

"Rather you didn't. Just tell me if it looks like the one you had in your vehicle."

Tom put his hands behind his back and narrowed his eyes as he looked through the clear plastic. "Yes. You can see yourself it's the type supplied by American car manufacturers."

"Anything special about yours?"

"Daddy," interrupted Tommy, "remember when Andy spilled the paint that time and the jack was laying out in the driveway."

Tom looked at Goodley. "There was paint on the handle."

"What color?"

"Red," Tom answered. He pointed to a child's wagon in the driveway. "That color."

"So when we get the mud off this jack, we'll know if it's the one from your car."

"Wanna check now? The hose is right around back."

"Let's give Forensics a chance to go over it first."

Jennie didn't like the look on either man's face.

Chapter Twelve

Twenty-four hours later, Jennie sat in the yard with Kate, sipping iced tea and keeping an eye on the four children huddled around the swingset.

Kate asked, "What do you think they're talking about?"

"Finding that jack. It has to be on their minds." She held the cold glass to her forehead. "They're too young to understand this." She sighed and leaned back against the trunk of a gnarled oak, grateful for the shade provided by its wide-reaching branches. It was unusually hot for September, even for Memphis—too hot to be outside, really—but both she and Kate admitted the need to be close to their children. Jennie's fair skin was dotted with perspiration. She gathered her thick, dark hair into one hand, away from the back of her neck, and gazed up at the leaves, searching for some sign of a cooling breeze. She sensed Tommy leaving the other kids and walking toward her.

"Mom, tell me—"

"Please, honey, I've already told you everything I know."

"But you don't even know what I was going to say."

"I'm sorry." She reached for his hand, kissed the small, dirty fingertips, steeled herself, and asked, "What do you want to know?"

"Was Robin already dead or did she get killed in our car?"

Of course. He would worry about that, just as she did. She said, "No, she didn't get killed in our car," not sure if she was telling the truth. She felt certain the police must know, but they hadn't told her.

They were interrupted by a voice from the side of the house.

Tommy looked over his mother's shoulder. "Aunt Ellen's here," he said and left to rejoin the other kids.

Ellen approached, holding out a book. "I just finished this. Thought it might take your mind off things."

"Thanks. Want a glass of tea?"

"No. I can't stay." Ellen looked toward the street and said, "He's out there again."

"Goodley?" Kate asked.

"Of course she means Goodley," Jennie said. "Seems like he's always around. Clipboard in hand. Standing on someone's front step. Now, this business with the jack . . ." She swept one hand through the air, not bothering to finish the sentence.

"Have you heard yet whether it's yours?" Ellen asked.

"One and the same."

"Is it the murder weapon?"

Jennie shrugged. "They don't know one way or the other. They say the shape fits the profile, but there are no traces of blood or hair . . . or anything like that."

"You'd think there'd be something."

Jennie agreed, and in fact found it impossible to believe the police didn't know more than they were saying. She said, "Maybe they just don't want to tell us."

Ellen said, "I suppose that's possible."

"I have a feeling Goodley thinks it's the murder weapon. He's been in the neighborhood every day. He must've talked to everyone on the street by now."

Ellen, ever reasonable, said, "That's his job."

Jennie shot her a look that could kill, but refrained from saying what she felt: *You're supposed to be on my side.*

Kate said, "The sooner he finds the killer, the sooner this will be over."

Jennie glared at both of them. "He's not looking for the killer. He's looking for proof that I did it." Her eyes challenged them to disagree with her.

Ellen said, "Jennie, stop it. You're borrowing trouble. There's no reason to think he suspects you."

"Then why's he questioning all my neighbors?"

"They're Robin's neighbors too," Ellen pointed out.

"How about you?" Jennie asked Kate. "Do you think I'm borrowing trouble?" Before Kate could answer, she added, "I don't blame him. If I were in his place, I'd suspect me too."

Kate said, "I don't think he actually suspects you. That's a bit dramatic."

"Yes," Jennie said. "He does. And I'm not being dramatic." She looked at Ellen now. "You know what I think. I think he's trying to figure out my motive. And he can't. Why would I kill Robin? That's got him stumped. And it stumps me too."

"What do you mean?"

"Motive. Why would anyone want to kill Robin? She was a sweet kid. The only person I can think of is Brad. Especially after the funeral." She stopped a minute, adding, "Maybe Web. I have a feeling there's more there than meets the eye."

Ellen said, "I still can't get over the funeral. Brad showing up looking like that . . . like a wild man."

Jennie said, "He was obviously crazy about her."

"Still," Ellen said, "a little self-control—"

Jennie interrupted. "Another thing I can't figure out is when the jack appeared under that rock. The day after we found the body, I took a walk back there. In the woods, I mean. To sort of get myself together. When I came back, I sat on that rock a few minutes before I came in the house. I remember exactly where I was sitting, because I was watching the squirrels play. And my feet were right next to the spot where the jack was found. I couldn't have missed it. So somebody must have put the jack there after that. But who? And when?"

"Good question," Ellen said. "Do you have an answer?"

"No. But I'm sure Goodley's working on that one too. And, again, I'm the most logical culprit."

"Stop it, Jen," Kate said. "You'll drive yourself crazy."

Ellen changed the subject. "How's Tom holding up?"

Jennie shrugged. "Okay."

"This must be hard on him."

"It's hard on all of us."

Ellen persisted. "I know, but . . . well, Robin had such a crush on him. And you know how flattering that is to a man Tom's age."

Jennie raised her eyebrows and pulled down the corners of her mouth. "Meaning?"

"He's about to hit the big four-oh," Ellen said. "That's a tough age." She glanced at her watch. "I better go. I have to pick up Elizabeth at her piano lesson."

Jennie turned to Kate after Ellen had gone, fluttered a hand to fan herself, and asked, "How's that for a hit and run?"

"Don't pay any attention to her," Kate advised. "She has a thing about Tom herself."

"Don't be silly. They were friends in college, and then they worked together for a while. That's all."

"That's what they told you."

Chapter Thirteen

Jennie and Tom were treating themselves to a lazy Saturday morning in bed while the kids watched TV in the family room. Smokey stretched contentedly on Jennie's stomach, pinning her to the spot where she lay. Tom, propped on pillows beside her, frowned at a crossword puzzle.

She watched him, wondering if Kate could be right. Had there ever been anything between him and Ellen? "Must be a tough one," she said. "You usually finish those things in no time."

"Can't concentrate."

"That's understandable." She drew a figure eight with her finger over the head and around the ears of the cat. *How do I ask? It seems silly after all these years.* Finally, she decided straight-out was best and said, "How do you feel about Ellen?"

"She's okay," he mumbled, still frowning at the folded newspaper.

"Put that down. I want to talk. How do you feel about her?"

He searched her face before he laid the paper aside. "She's a little prissy for my taste, but as in-laws go—"

"She's more than an in-law to you."

"Okay. So we go way back."

"Did you ever—"

"What brought this on?" He moved closer and stroked her arm.

She had expected him to laugh at the question. "Something's wrong."

He leaned over and buried his face in her hair. "I love you."

The tone of his voice had changed. *There* is *something wrong.* She felt a tightness in her chest just above her heart. *What did I miss?* She said, "Everything between us happened so fast. You and Ellen?"

"We were friends. Period."

"That's what I've always assumed but, to tell the truth, I didn't really think about it."

"So why now? Eleven years later?"

"Something Kate said yesterday."

"Kate?"

She felt a buzz of energy flowing through his fingers into her arm. "Kate said something. I don't remember what exactly. Anyway, she seemed to think the two of you . . ." She paused, waiting. Tom was lying beside her, their bodies just touching. The words they had been speaking still hung in the air. These things she could place, but something else, some subtle, ghostlike essence, hovered just at the edge of her perception. She braced herself, determined to understand what was happening.

Tom removed his hand from her arm, rolled over, and lay on his back, staring at the ceiling.

She studied his profile, touched, as always, by its sharply etched perfection.

Artificial laughter from the television in the next room intruded on the silence that was growing between them. "Awesome!" Andy's high, sweet voice broke through the shrill pattern of sound from the box.

Tom got up and closed the bedroom door.

"There is something. Something I have to tell you."

"About Ellen?"

"No," he said, "Not Ellen." He sat down on the bed and reached for her hand. "You know I love you. You do know that, don't you?"

She didn't pull her hand away, but neither did she return the pressure of his fingers. She left his question unanswered.

He repeated, "You know I love you." His voice cracked as he continued, "If only I could go back and—"

She removed her hand from his and lifted the cat so she could sit up. "Who?" The word came out as a whisper.

No answer.

"Tell me who. I don't want to know anything else but— Tell me!"

And, most of all, why is it bothering you right now?

Still no answer.

"Who was it?"

He looked away, swallowing rapidly. "This . . . everything that's happened—"

"Stop stalling."

"It had nothing to do with . . . the murder."

"Why should I th—" She stopped, looked at his face, and she knew. "It was Robin."

The sounds of the television and the boys' intermittent laughter and bickering were still there, but were now muffled by the closed door and the pounding in her temples.

"You and Robin?" Jennie could feel her voice rising, going out of control. She panicked when she felt his hands on her arms. "Don't!" she shrieked, scrambling to the other side of the bed, beyond his reach.

"Jennie, I wanted to tell you. You don't know—"

She turned her face and put her hands to her ears to block him out, but the warm, early-morning scent of him was still there. There was no blocking that. In the jumble of his words, she heard "the kids," and knew she had to listen. When she looked back toward him, she realized that Tommy and Andy had come into the room. They stood just inside the doorway, watching her with anxious faces. Their father was standing by the bed, leaning toward her. Andy looked ready to cry.

"Mommy, what's wrong?" Tommy asked.

Andy went to his father, who picked him up.

"What happened?" Tommy persisted, crawling onto the bed with her. Andy wriggled out of his father's arms and joined his mother and brother on the bed.

Jennie wanted to reassure them, but could find no voice. All she could do was hold them close to her. She used a corner of the sheet to wipe the tears from Andy's face.

Tom spoke for her. "Mommy had a bad dream, guys."

"But she wasn't asleep," Tommy said. His childish mouth puckered with concentration as he looked from one parent to the other.

"She read us a story when we first woke up," Andy reminded him. "Before we watched TV."

Tom looked at Jennie, appealing silently for help. As much as she wanted to deny him, she had to reassure the kids.

How? What do I say to them? She looked around the room, finally focusing on the book on her bedside table. She picked it up for them to see. "I read until late last night and I was still sleepy this morning. So, when you guys went to watch TV, and Daddy was working his crosswork puzzle, I took a little catnap." She forced herself to smile into their trusting faces. "That's when I had the bad dream."

"Tell you what, guys," Tom said. "You go watch one more cartoon, give Mommy a little time to pull herself together, and then we'll all go out to brunch. Okay?"

Tommy twisted away from his mother so he could see her face. Then he looked back at his father. "I think we better stay with Mom."

"I'm okay," Jennie forced herself to say. "Really I am. Daddy's right. I just need a little time. Brunch sounds like a great idea."

Tommy looked doubtful, but he took his brother's hand and led him from the room.

"Okay," Jennie said when they were alone. "Let's hear it."

"Robin—"

"She's a child!"

"She's eighteen."

"Still, I can't believe you would do such a thing."

"I didn't 'do such a thing'! She . . . it just happened."

"Oh, come on! Things don't just happen!"

"Remember last summer when she had a crush on me?"

Jennie watched him through narrowed eyes.

"Everyone kidded me about it. Even you."

"And you expect me to believe she chased you around the bedroom? Or was it the backseat of a car?"

When he answered, Jennie heard his voice, but the words were meaningless, as senseless and insistent as the cartoon voices that penetrated the closed bedroom door. "Not a car . . . your father . . . heart attack . . . missed you." She got out of bed, went to the window, and stood looking out at the too-bright morning, avoiding her husband's reflection in the glass.

"Aren't you going to let me explain?" he asked.

"I don't want to hear it." Then, anger breaking through, "I trusted you!"

"Please, Jennie, I need to tell you."

"You need!"

"It's not what you think."

"You don't know what I think. You don't know me at all. And I sure don't know you. I thought I did, but—"

"Jennie, listen. Just listen. After what's happened . . . What if the police find out? We should have a plan."

"A plan?" She heard her voice rising again, and paused a moment to gain control. "Leave me out of your plans."

"What about the kids? What if they find out?"

"Fine time to think about that."

"Should we tell them?"

"Of course not!"

"What if they hear about it from someone else?"

She looked at him, stunned. "Who else knows?"

He hesitated. "Probably no one. I didn't tell anyone and I doubt Robin would have. But with this investigation . . . if the police find out . . ." He put his hands to his face, pulled them away, and took a deep breath. "Or the press. We have to think about the possibility."

Looking at his reflection in the windowpane, she saw his shoulders slumped, the proud, upright squareness of him diminished. That frightened her and blunted the edge of her anger. She went back to the bed and sat down beside him, avoiding his touch.

"Okay. Let's hear it."

He nodded, began, "It's not really important . . . well, important, yes, but not in the way you think."

She watched his face, thinking, *He loves me. I know he does love me,* and forced herself to listen.

"In May when your father had the heart attack. You stayed with your mother while he was in the hospital and Robin stayed here to look after the kids."

"That's when?"

He nodded.

"Are you trying to tell me she decided to sleep with you instead of the guest room?"

"No. That's not what happened at all!"

Jennie moved from the bed to a chair in the farthest corner of the room. "What did happen?"

"I came home early one day. Robin was alone in the house playing the piano. Ellen had taken the boys to a movie to give Robin a breather. When I came in I heard music—" He stopped to look at his wife and took a deep breath before he continued, "Rachmaninoff. The piece you were playing the first time I saw you."

"That's supposed to make everything all right?"

"I didn't say that."

"Not in so many words."

He stood up and paced the length of the room before he spoke again, "Anyway we were alone in the house together and . . . Jennie, please, you have to believe me. It would never have happened if I hadn't missed you so much."

She said nothing.

"You know I love you."

"Did you kill her?"

"No. I swear to you I did not."

Jennie reached for the small pillow in the chair beside her and held it between crossed arms, studying her husband. "That day, what time did you get to Seattle?" she finally asked.

"What're you getting at? You know—"

"Can I see the ticket stubs?"

"I don't have them."

"Hotel receipt?"

He ran his hands through his hair, and turned in a circle—an animal in a too-small cage.

Jennie persisted. "Anything?"

"There isn't anything. Not where I can get to it."

"But you save everything. Always."

"I left my briefcase on the plane, and it hasn't been returned yet. I know that's not like me, but—"

"Not like you? I'll say! Most of the time, you act like the riches of the Orient are in that briefcase. This time you left it on a plane?"

"Jeez, Jennie! It was a rough two days. My tail was draggin' when I got hit with all this."

"Why didn't you say something before?"

"I don't know. It didn't seem important."

"How can you say that?"

"I meant the briefcase isn't important. Compared to . . . well, what you'd been through."

"So there's nothing to prove when you arrived in Seattle?"

He spread his hands wide and looked at her.

Chapter Fourteen

Goodley drove slowly down the avenue of towering oaks and turned when he saw a bronze plaque proclaiming BARRONS MANOR attached to one of the stone pillars flanking a long, gracefully winding driveway. The house at the driveway's end rose white and stately from the cool green of shaded lawn and lush beds of ivy. Large urns filled with impatiens in shades of pink and lavender occupied the spaces between the columns of the veranda. He noted these details and, after ringing the bell, continued to examine the house. He was studying the intricate scrollwork surrounding the entryway when the door opened to reveal a middle-aged woman in a crisp uniform.

He held up a leather wallet containing his identification. "Lieutenant Weston Goodley, River County Homicide Department."

The woman scrutinized the picture on the badge, and then his face. "I'll get Mrs. Barrons."

"It's Webster Barrons I'm here to see."

She nodded without comment and disappeared into the dim interior, leaving Goodley standing outside, still holding the badge up for inspection. By the time he had the wallet back in his pocket, another woman had appeared at the door. She was pudgy and as short as a child, despite the high-heeled pumps she wore.

"I'm Leda Barrons," she told him.

"I'd like to speak to Webster Barrons."

"I'm his mother."

Goodley waited for her to add more. When she did not, he asked, "Is your son at home?"

"No."

"Do you expect him back soon?"

"Webster's down in Oxford. He attends the University of Mississippi."

"I need to speak to him in connection with the death of Robin Langley."

"If you'd like to make an appointment—"

The roar of an approaching engine drowned out her next words. A red Porsche convertible slid to a stop in the driveway. When the driver emerged, Goodley recognized the young man who had stood with Joe and Gladys Langley outside the church the day of the funeral.

Leda Barrons was obviously flustered. "Why, good heavens, here he is now." When the boy joined them at the front door, she said, "Web, darling, this is Lieutenant Goodley. He's the policeman who's investigating Robin's death. He wants to speak to you."

The young man had inherited his mother's short, blocky build and had to tip his head back to look Goodley in the eye. "Sure, anything I can do to help. Do you have any suspects yet?" Eyes the color of a summer sky made Webster Barrons seem younger than his eighteen years, and very vulnerable.

Goodley's shrug was noncommittal.

"Let's not stand out here," Mrs. Barrons said. "Please come in, Lieutenant Goodley." She was gracious in the manner of one conveying a great favor to a lesser being.

Goodley followed mother and son through the foyer, past the beautifully carved walnut staircase. Their footsteps were muffled by a thick Oriental runner that covered the center area of the hall, leaving burnished oak floors exposed on either side. They led him into a comfortable room furnished with three deep leather couches grouped in front of a walk-in fireplace. The walls were lined with floor-to-ceiling shelves. Interspersed with books were athletic trophies and framed photographs, most of them showing Web's face at various ages.

"Please sit down, Lieutenant," said Leda Barrons, indicating the couch directly opposite the fireplace. She waited until her son chose a seat and then sat next to him.

Goodley noted the reading material on the large square table in front of the couch: several issues of *The Cotton Broker* and a glossy-covered book with *Mansions Along the Mississippi* printed in gothic letters under a picture of a columned building seen through an avenue of live oaks.

"How can we help you, Lieutenant?" asked Mrs. Barrons.

"My questions are really for your son."

"Of course," she said stiffly. "The 'we' was rhetorical."

Turning his attention to Web, Goodley asked, "Tell me about your relationship with Miss Langley."

"He was—" Again, it was Leda who spoke.

Web shook his mother's hand off his arm. "Please, I can handle this." He said to Goodley, "We went out a few times."

"Went out a few times?" echoed Goodley. "I noticed you were sitting with the family at the funeral. That would seem to indicate a more serious relationship."

"Really, Lieutenant, don't you think they were a little young for a serious relationship?"

"Mother!"

"Perhaps I could speak to your son alone."

Leda studied Goodley's face a few minutes and finally said, "Should our lawyer be present?"

"If you feel that's necessary, we can schedule an appointment with your attorney present. However, I'd like to point out that I'm not charging your son with a crime. I just want to talk to him about Miss Langley." The police lieutenant didn't blink, didn't miss a beat as he spoke.

"It's okay," Web assured his mother. "Let's not make a bigger deal out of this than it is."

The silence that followed was broken when the young man asked, "Do we have anything in the house to eat, Mom? I'm starving."

Mrs. Barrons looked from her son to Goodley, and then back, before she answered, "I'll have Dorothea make you a sandwich."

"Sorry about that," Web said after his mother left the room. The blue eyes glowed with sincerity.

Goodley seemed not to notice. "Tell me about your relationship with Miss Langley."

"We were friends."

Goodley tapped lightly on the clipboard with his pen. "You said you went out a few times. Does that mean you were dating?"

"No, we just hung out together."

"Other people seem to believe there was more to it than that."

"We were just friends." Web's fingers were clinching, unclinching, as he spoke. "Why do people always say 'just friends' as though friendship is nothing?"

"Was she dating anyone?"

"Not 'til Wilson came on the scene."

"When was that?"

"Late last winter. Maybe early spring. I don't remember exactly."

"Tell me about Brad Wilson coming on the scene. Your recollection of what happened."

Web shot Goodley a quick look before he answered. "Have you talked to him yet?"

Goodley indicated that he had.

Web glanced toward the door through which his mother had disappeared before he answered in a much lower voice, "I guess he told you they met at that place up in River County. Southern Lites. One night when I took her there."

Goodley nodded again.

Web continued, glancing again toward the door, "Did he tell you I had a little too much to drink that night?"

Another nod.

"Well, I admit I did. But not all that much. Robin just overreacted. Really freaked. She refused to let me drive her home."

"But you had been drinking?"

A cautious nod.

"Even had too much to drink?"

"Maybe a little."

"Tell me what happened."

"We had a fight. Robin wanted to drive. She thought I couldn't. When I wouldn't let her, she refused to go home with me."

"So you left her there?"

"What was I supposed to do? She wouldn't get in the car with me."

"Why didn't you let her drive?"

"I told you. It wasn't necessary."

"Didn't you worry? Leaving her like that?"

Web shrugged but did not speak.

"After that night? The friendship continued?"

"Yes."

"And Brad Wilson? Where did he fit into the picture?"

"Robin saw a lot of him."

"How did you feel about that?"

"It worried me some."

"Worried you? Why?"

"I thought she was in over her head."

"Why did you think that?"

"Well, sometimes I'd take her someplace and he'd just show up and she'd act kind of nervous, but she always invited him to join us and sometimes . . . all the time the last few months . . . she'd tell me he was going to take her home and they'd go off together." He hesitated, clinching and unclinching the fist, gripping his knee. "She was using me so her parents wouldn't know she was seeing him." He looked directly at Goodley. "I knew that."

"This didn't bother you?"

He shrugged. "I told you. Robin and I were friends. We had our ups and downs, but we were still friends."

"What do you think of Brad Wilson?"

"I think he's scary as hell."

"Do you think he's capable of murder?" Goodley almost whispered the question.

"Probably." Web stared into space, clinching his jaw.

Goodley made no attempt to break the silence.

"Have you talked to Emma yet?" Web asked abruptly.

"Emma?" Goodley looked through his pages of notes. "Who's she?"

Web said, "That crazy old flower lady."

"I don't know who you mean."

"She lives in that house on the highway, right at the corner where you turn off to Wilson's shack. The place the papers are calling Oz. Just looks like a jungle to me."

"Who is she? What does she have to do with this?"

"She's really tight with Brad. And I don't think she liked him being so crazy about Robin."

"But who is she?" Goodley repeated.

"I don't know exactly. I don't think they're related or anything, but I know she's always doing things for him. Robin told me about it. The old lady made curtains for his house. Little ruffled jobbies." Web stopped to laugh. "In that old shack he lives in. And she even went down there and planted flowers in front and made a little garden for him."

"What makes you think she didn't like Miss Langley?"

"Robin told me Emma didn't like her. She was right too. I saw that firsthand."

"Oh?"

"One time Robin got me to take her up to Wilson's place. Only he wasn't home. So we stopped by this Emma's and asked her if she knew where he was." Web stopped speaking when his mother came in with a tray.

Leda Barrons said, "Dorothea had some of your favorite. Honey-baked ham." She placed the tray on the table before him and started to sit down.

"Mom, I can handle this myself."

She studied her son with furrowed brow for a few seconds, but left the room without protest.

"Thanks for the sandwich," he called after her.

Goodley waited until he heard a door open and then close in another part of the house before he prompted, "You say you took Miss Langley to Emma's looking for Brad Wilson?"

"Yeah. Robin called me one morning. Really upset. Asked if I'd do her a favor. I said sure. Then, when I picked her up, she told me she needed a ride up to Wilson's place. She didn't have a car and she didn't want her parents to know about it."

"Any idea what it was about?"

"She wouldn't tell me. She said she had to talk to Brad. She had to tell him something. I tried to talk her out of it. But, like I said, she was really upset. She wouldn't listen to me. Just kept saying she had to talk to Brad. So I finally gave in and drove her up there. That's when I saw where he lives." Web stopped speaking and looked at Goodley, as though waiting for his comment.

Goodley said nothing.

Web continued, "Anyway, he wasn't home. And Robin said maybe

Emma would know where he was. So we went there. That's the place with all the flowers."

"When did this happen?"

"I can't give you a date. Sometime in the spring."

"Would you say shortly before graduation?"

"That's about right."

"And Emma seemed hostile toward Miss Langley?"

Web took his time. "Yeah, I'd say hostile is a good word. She sure didn't want to tell her where Brad was."

"Do you think she knew?"

Web shrugged. "How could I tell what she knew? But I can tell you this. She was not happy that Robin was there looking for Brad."

"Can you tell me anything else about this Emma?"

"No. That's the only time I ever saw her. But she seemed strange. Weird. Like somebody I wouldn't want to cross." Web took a bite of the sandwich.

Goodley made some notes and waited for Web to finish chewing before he asked, "Can you tell me where you were the morning of August twenty-eighth?" When he did not respond immediately, Goodley prompted, "It was a Monday."

"I know what day you're talking about. The day Robin was killed. I was taking some things down to Oxford, getting ready to start school."

"Was anyone with you?"

"No." Web watched while Goodley made a note of this. "Is that a problem, Lieutenant? Do I need an alibi?"

Goodley ignored the question. "What can you tell me about Miss Langley's relationship with Mrs. Connors?"

"Oh, they got along great. Robin admired her. Her husband too. Talked all the time about what a great couple they were. At least she used to. Lately she'd stopped saying anything about them."

"Any idea why?"

"No."

Goodley nodded, and said in a soft voice, "Let's get back to your relationship with Miss Langley."

Web bristled, holding the plate with the half-eaten sandwich in one hand while the fingers of the other hand gripped his knee, turning the knuckles white. "We were friends. I'd even say she was my best friend. Someone I could talk to."

"What about Brad Wilson?" Goodley was studying the young man openly now.

He sat rigidly upright, staring back at the policeman. He didn't answer.

"What about Wilson?" repeated Goodley. "Did Robin plan to marry him?" Goodley asked the second question sharply, without giving Web time to answer the first.

Web gave a short laugh. "She talked about it. But I knew she wouldn't."

"How could you know that?"

"You've seen him. Seen where he lives. What did he have that a girl like her would want?"

Leda Barrons came into the room. "Lieutenant Goodens . . ."

"Goodley, Mother. His name is Goodley."

"Sorry." She looked briefly at the lieutenant and turned to her son. "I've just spoken to your father on the telephone, and he insists that our attorney be present at any interview which Mr. Goodley . . ." She paused as she emphasized the second syllable, and continued, "desires with any member of this family."

Chapter Fifteen

I know something's bothering you."

"I appreciate your concern, but . . ." Jennie began shoving the stack of folders into a carry-all. "Look, I'm running late." She finally let her nervous hands rest and looked at Kate. "Okay, you're right. There is something, but I have to work it out myself." She went back to packing the files and old magazines into the tote bag until it looked ready to burst. "I need a little space right now."

"Okay. But if you—"

She breathed a sigh of relief when the telephone cut short Kate's words and ran to answer its insistent summons. "Hello."

"Mrs. Connors?"

The voice was pleasantly accented.

"This is Edward Pynchon."

The name, with each syllable crisply pronounced, tugged at Jennie's memory.

"You're—"

"A dealer in old recordings and books," the clear voice prompted.

"Of course. From the flea market. Sorry it took me so long to remember. It's just . . . well, a lot has happened since that morning."

"I read about the unfortunate incident in the newspaper and wondered if it was the same Jennifer Connors. Then I saw you on the telly with your family."

"Uh . . . the day of the funeral?"

"Yes." He paused, adding, "Can you come to Barney's today?"

"I have to work until two today. Will you be there tomorrow?"

There was another pause. "Sometimes it's not a good idea to put things off."

Jennie finally convinced Pynchon that she could not possibly drive up to Barney's until the following day.

Kate mouthed "see you later" and slipped quietly out the door.

Later that morning, Jennie thought back over her brief conversation with the book dealer as she sorted through a box of player piano rolls. She selected "In the Shade of the Old Apple Tree," and went looking for an aide.

"Please," she coaxed the young woman she found lounging by the vending machine, "I just need five minutes. It'll be easy. They all love to sing along with these old songs . . . and I picked one of their favorites."

She stayed in the recreation room long enough to get them started. "I'll be right back. Just have to make one quick phone call."

"Hi," she said when she heard Kate's voice at the other end of the line. "Got a minute?"

"Sure. Glad you called. You were pretty grim this morning."

"I know," Jennie said. "That's why I'm calling . . . thought I might buy back your friendship with lunch."

"I never pass up lunch."

"One thing though, Kate. No questions. There's something I have to work out . . . and I have to do it myself."

The next morning the doorbell rang a little earlier than Jennie expected. "Come on in. Door's unlocked," she called, and went on talking without looking up to see who it was. "You're early, but I'm almost ready. Just have to make a quick call to check on things at Riverview. It'll only take—" She dropped the phone when she saw Goodley.

"You said come on in."

"I know. I was expecting . . . never mind." She bent to pick up the phone, placed the receiver squarely in its cradle, and squared her shoulders before she faced him. "What can I do for you?"

He handed her a cream-colored business card. "Tell me about this."

She looked down at the small rectangle, which read EDWARD PYNCHON—DEALER IN OLD BOOKS & RECORDINGS, and back up at the policeman. "I don't understand."

Goodley's eyes did not leave her face as he reached to turn the card over in her hand. Her name and phone number were written on the back. She recognized the upward slant of her own handwriting.

He said, "Describe your relationship with Mr. Pynchon."

"There's no relationship. I met him once . . . at Barney's . . . the day the car . . . and Robin—" Jennie realized she was babbling, paused, and said, "I've told you all that before."

He took the card from her. "Explain to me exactly what transpired between you and Mr. Pynchon."

Something in his manner caused prickles on the back of Jennie's neck. She took her time answering. "That day . . . I mean the day the car was stolen . . . I gave him my phone number so he could call me if he found any records like I was looking for. Then he called yesterday and asked me to come up there. I'm on my way to see him now."

"Did he say why?"

"I guess he found some records for me."

"You're not sure?"

"Sure of what?" The question came out sharper than she had intended. *Don't antagonize him.* She took a deep breath and tried to remember Mr. Pynchon's exact words. She couldn't.

"No, I'm not sure," she said.

She and Goodley were standing in the foyer, with the door partially open. She glanced over his shoulder and saw Kate in the driveway, looking from the policeman's car to the open door. "Kate's waiting for me," she said. "Should I tell her to come back later?"

"Tell her to come in."

When Kate joined them, Jennie led both her and Goodley into the living room. Goodley acknowledged Kate's presence with a curt nod before he turned again to Jennie.

"You guessed that he had some records for you. Did he say that?"

"I don't remember exactly what he said. I was in a hurry. Getting ready . . . anyway, he had already told me he'd call if he found records I could use." Then, because Goodley seemed to expect more, she added, "What else could it be?"

After what seemed a long time, he said, "Mr. Pynchon's been in a car accident."

She remembered the slight, dapper Englishman, his obvious pride in his record collection, his eagerness to help, and sat down. "Is he dead?"

Goodley shook his head.

"Thank goodness for that. How badly hurt is he?"

"His condition is listed as guarded."

"Is he going to be all right?"

"It's too soon to tell." Goodley held the cream-colored card aloft in two fingers. "This was in his pocket. The officer who responded to the call found it. He passed it along to me. Said he thought I'd be interested." He turned to Kate. "Were you going to see Mr. Pynchon too?"

She nodded.

"Were you looking for records?"

"No. I was just going along to keep Jennie company."

He looked at Jennie. "What time was the phone call?"

"About eight o'clock yesterday morning." Jennie looked at Kate for confirmation.

"That's about right," Kate said.

Goodley made a note on his clipboard. "What time was your appointment?" he asked.

"This morning. No special time. It wasn't really an appointment. Nothing that formal."

Goodley tapped his pen on the clipboard and looked at Jennie for a long moment. Finally he asked, "Was anyone else present when you took the call?"

"I was," Kate said.

"Then you heard the conversation?"

"Just Jennie's side of it."

"Anything you can add to what she told me?"

"No."

Goodley had remained standing during the interview. He now seated himself in the chair directly across the room from Jennie and asked her, "Did Pynchon sound different to you when you spoke to him yesterday?"

"Different from what? I'd only spoken to him once before."

"Did he sound agitated?"

"I couldn't tell. I was in the middle of things . . . on my way to work . . . trying to get out of the house. I didn't pay that much attention."

"You had never met him before that morning . . . the day your car was stolen?"

"That's right."

"No other contact between that morning and the phone call yesterday?"

"No."

"Where were you yesterday afternoon?"

"I was at home."

"Anyone with you?"

"No. I was alone. My mother took the boys to see the fox cubs at the petting zoo."

"And you?" He turned to Kate.

"I took my daughter to the dentist," she told him.

There were a few more questions, but Jennie had the feeling Goodley had lost interest.

"It was an accident, wasn't it?" she asked.

He didn't answer right away. When he finally spoke, he sounded almost as if he were talking to himself. "It looked like an accident."

Chapter Sixteen

Jennie watched from the window until Goodley's Jetta was out of sight. "Come on," she said to Kate. "Let's get going!"

"Going? Where?"

"Barney's, of course." And, with that, Jennie headed for the door. "Come on. We have to be back before the kids get home. And we're looking at a forty-five-minute drive each way."

Kate said, "You already know he's not there."

"I'm going to look around. See if I can figure out what's up."

Kate looked skeptical, but she followed Jennie to the car. Once they were on their way she said, "This is not a good idea. Remember what happened last time you decided to play Miss Marple."

"Meaning?"

"Meaning you went looking for a stolen car and found a whole lot more."

"How much more can there be?"

"Robin's dead. That old Englishman . . . he's alive . . . but apparently not by much. That's something to think about."

Jennie refused to be deterred. "There's something fishy about that accident."

"Let Goodley handle it. He's the pro."

"As long as he's convinced that I'm the killer—"

Kate looked ready to protest, but Jennie stopped her. "I don't think he's a monster. I've gotten over that. I figure if I can find something . . . anything . . . to point him in another direction, he'll check it out. And I'll be off the hook. Mr. Pynchon must have seen something. Something he thinks I should know. He was upset that I couldn't come yesterday. I want to know why."

"You make it sound personal."

If you only knew. But Jennie wasn't ready to share Tom's secret, not even with Kate. She took another deep breath before she spoke again. "And, to tell the truth, I'd like you along as my alibi in case anything else happens. Did you see Goodley's face when I told him I was home alone yesterday afternoon?"

"Okay. Count me in."

"Thanks," Jennie said. She kept the conversation general, safely away from the murder, until they came to the sign announcing BARNSTABLE'S FLEA MARKET & BAR B Q SHACK.

"Now what?" Kate asked when they got out of the car. When Jennie didn't answer immediately, Kate wrinkled her nose and suggested, "We can start with lunch. That barbecue's calling my name."

"I want to check Mr. Pynchon's table first."

Kate sighed impressively, but made no other objection.

They walked past the screened pavilion where the food was served, into the flea market area, through aisles formed by tables heaped with an assortment of picked-over merchandise, the wallflowers of the summer season. A few customers strolled idly among the tables, occasionally stopping to look, but rarely bothering to ask a price. Even the vendors seemed half-hearted in their offerings. Most of them sat in lawn chairs, fanning themselves with folded newspapers or magazines.

"We're in luck," Jennie said as they approached the row of tables at the edge of the field. "Someone's there."

Perched on the high stool where Jennie had last seen Edward Pynchon was a woman reading a magazine. They exchanged cautious nods and Jennie began looking through boxes of record albums. The woman tucked a tendril of perspiration-damp hair behind her ear and watched Jennie through narrowed eyes. "Need help?" she asked. She got off the stool and came closer.

"I'm not sure," Jennie answered. She flipped album after album forward, quickly but thoroughly examining the contents of each box. When she finished she turned to Kate. "Nothing here. So it wasn't records." She held out her hand to the woman and said, "I'm Jennifer Connors. I was supposed to meet Mr. Pynchon here this morning." She thought she saw a flicker of interest cross the impassive face. Hoping to bring it to life, she added, "The murdered girl . . . it was my car they found her in. I think the police believe there's a connection between the murder and the accident."

The woman seemed to consider this. "Maybe my father can help you. Wait here." She left them and went to speak to an elderly couple seated at a nearby table. When she came back, she said, "They'll watch Edward's things while we go talk to my father. Not many customers anyway." Finally she smiled. "I'm Lydia Barnstable."

Jennie and Kate followed Lydia, retracing their steps through the aisles of tables to the screened pavilion near the entrance. Unlike the grounds of the flea market, the food pavilion was filled with people. The pungent aroma that had been calling to Kate was particularly eloquent in here. Lydia led them into the kitchen at the far end of the pavilion.

"Hey, Pop," she said to the large man standing in front of the stove.

"What you want, Duchess?" he asked, concentrating on the sizzling skillet in front of him.

"Somebody wants to talk to you." When he didn't answer, she added, "About Edward."

He looked over his shoulder. His expression changed when he saw Jennie standing next to his daughter. He handed his spatula to a thick-set man working at the counter next to him. "You take over here . . . don't let these tomatoes burn." He wiped his hands on the apron that covered his front from chest to knee, studying Jennie and Kate as he did so. His eyes were direct and appraising, so intense that Jennie couldn't tell if he was smiling or frowning. His mouth was almost hidden in a beard that looked like a bristling silver brush.

Lydia said, "This is my father, Lucas Barnstable."

"Hello, Mr. Barnstable," Jennie said, holding out her hand. "I'm Jennifer Connors."

"Call me Barney," he said, taking her hand. "Everybody else does. And I know who you are. Saw your picture in the newspaper."

Jennie grimaced at the mention of her notoriety. Kate stepped forward and introduced herself.

"Pop," Lydia said, after he had shaken Kate's hand, "the police think Edward's accident might be connected to that murder."

Barney studied Jennie for a few seconds before his round face split into a smile. "My guess is you want more than the secret of my barbecue sauce."

"I'm not sure it's more than that, but it's different than that."

He laughed aloud, a booming, irresistible deluge of sound.

"Mr. Pynchon called me yesterday," Jennie told him when the laughter subsided. "Asked me to meet him here."

Barney nodded, encouraging her to say more.

"I thought he had some records for me, but . . ."

"Now you think it was something else," he finished for her. "Why?"

"Because I looked through every record on the table and there was nothing there. Nothing he would have called me about."

"Let's go out here where we can talk." He opened the door and stepped aside to let Jennie and Kate pass. Lydia excused herself. Barney, Jennie, and Kate sat down at a picnic table near the door. "What do you want from me?" he asked.

"I don't know," Jennie admitted. "This morning, I was just about to leave the house when Lieutenant Goodley came by. He told me about the accident. Only I got the impression he doesn't think it was really an accident."

"Did he say that?"

"Not in so many words. But Goodley's a homicide detective. So I started to wonder. And I came to check it out. Your daughter said I should talk to you."

"I see." He rubbed his hands over the brushlike beard.

"Do you think it was an accident?"

Barney didn't answer. His eyes seemed to be evading Jennie's as he stared over her head. When he looked back, he pointed to a table in the far corner of the pavilion. "See that lady over there?"

"The one reading the magazine?"

He nodded. "She's the one who found him after the accident."

Kate spoke up. "That's funny. I noticed her when we came in. Had the feeling I'd seen her before."

"Really?" Jennie looked at her friend and then at the woman. "Me too. But I don't know where."

When Barney got up and started toward the woman, Jennie and

Kate followed. As they approached, Jennie noticed that the reading material was not a magazine but a seed catalog. The woman was tall, very slender, and, although dressed in work clothes, had an air of self-possessed elegance about her. She and Barney greeted each other with a nod.

"This is Jennie. And this is Kate." Barney indicated each of them with a flourish as he spoke her name.

"And," he said as he moved around the table to stand behind the woman, "this is Emma." He sat down next to Emma and motioned to Jennie and Kate to sit down on the other side of the table.

"Sorry to interrupt your lunch," Jennie said.

"I'm just finishing."

"Edward called this young lady," Barney nodded in Jennie's direction. "Asked her to meet him here this morning."

Jennie said, "Barney said you were the one who found him. I mean . . . after the accident."

"I know what you mean."

Jennie looked at Emma, hoping that she would say more. When she didn't, Jennie asked, "Do you think it was really an accident?"

"Why wouldn't I?"

"I got the feeling Lieutenant Goodley doesn't think so."

"It's his job to suspect the worst."

"Mr. Pynchon had a card with my name and phone number in his pocket. And I'm the one whose car—"

"I know. Saw your picture in the paper. On TV too, when I watched the news with Edward."

"Goodley acts like he thinks I'm responsible for the accident."

"Are you?"

Jennie was becoming more uncomfortable by the second and knew it showed. She had the feeling Emma was enjoying it and wondered why.

"Are you responsible for the accident?" Emma persisted.

"No."

"Then you don't have anything to worry about."

"Do you think—"

"Doesn't matter what I think." With that, Emma turned and walked away, straight-backed, head held high.

As if to answer Jennie's question, Barney said, "Edward always drove real slow. Said that was the only way he could keep track of where he was since Americans drive on the wrong side of the road. Everybody kidded him about it." He paused and looked after the departing Emma. "Especially her."

"So she knew him," Jennie said. "She wasn't just a stranger who happened by."

"Everybody knows everybody in River County."

"Were they friends?"

"Yeah. Good friends. Two loners who hit it off. Neither one had much patience with folks who followed the herd."

Jennie said, "So you're saying Mr. Pynchon didn't have a lot of friends. Did he have enemies?"

"No, no, no." Barney held up his hand. "You got it all wrong. Everybody liked him. He wasn't much for socializing, but he had friends. If he knew somebody needed help, he was first in line to help 'em out." Before Jennie could ask another question, he said, "How 'bout I treat you ladies to a plate of the best barbecue in the South? You wait right here." And he was gone.

Too restless to sit, Jennie got up and wandered around the pavilion while they waited for him to come back. She stopped to read a poster nailed to one of the supports. "Hey," she called to Kate, "come here." When Kate joined her, she pointed to the poster. "Southern Lites. That's where Brad works."

"So?"

She tapped the bottom half of the poster. "That's his play schedule."

Kate rolled her eyes. "I hope you're not thinking what I think you are."

Chapter Seventeen

Goodley noted the name, E. Malich, stenciled on a mailbox almost obscured by purple blooms and green tentacles. When he stepped from the car, he saw a straw hat that seemed to float just above one of the many blocks of brilliant color. No human form was visible. The hat was the only indication that one might be present.

"Hello." He pulled a wallet with his identification from a pocket and approached the patch of scarlet before which the hat floated. "Weston Goodley, River County Homicide."

The hat tipped back. Wisps of soft, gray curls spilled out beneath the wide brim. A pair of lively, inquisitive eyes looked directly into Goodley's face, ignoring the badge.

"Emma Malich," the woman said. She sat back on her heels, looking him over. When she stood, he was surprised to discover she was almost as tall as he was. He judged her age to be somewhere in the mid-fifties.

She studied his face a few minutes before she smiled and held out her hand.

Goodley held up his ID again.

"Put that thing away. I know who you are." Her wave of dismissal was so abrupt that he thought for a moment she was going to slap the badge out of his hand.

"I'd like to talk to you about Mr. Pynchon's accident," he said when the wallet was safely back in his pocket.

"May as well do it over a cup of tea." Without waiting for a response, she turned toward the house.

Goodley watched her bend to pick up a pair of gardening gloves from the steps.

94

"Gift from my niece," she said, waving the gloves.

"Nice."

"I start out wearing them every morning," she explained as they entered her home through the side door, "but they always end up on the steps or the path." She led him through a hall and into the kitchen, where she began filling the kettle, all the while keeping up a steady stream of comments in her pleasantly rough-edged voice. "Shame to waste a gift, but I love the feel of dirt on my hands." The roughness left her voice as the last words were spoken.

When Goodley cleared his throat, she half-turned and looked at him over her shoulder. "Have a seat."

He sat in one of the chairs beside a wooden table filled with a clutter of potted plants, stacks of garden catalogs, and packets of seeds.

"Tea'll be ready in a minute or two." She continued to move around the kitchen.

He cleared his throat again.

"You got something to say, just say it. Don't worry about waiting for me to sit, 'cause I never do."

"I have some questions about Edward Pynchon's accident."

"I know. You told me that first thing."

"What can you tell me about it?"

"Everything's in the accident report I filled out."

Goodley said, "I've talked to a lot of people who knew Pynchon and were familiar with his driving habits. None of them think, slow as he drove, he'd run into a tree hard enough to smash up a car like that, especially that old Cadillac of his. Thing was built like a tank."

"I came along after it happened, reported it, didn't leave anything out."

"You a friend of Mr. Pynchon?"

"Edward. Just call him Edward. I hate formality. Think it's phony. Yes, we're friends." These comments were delivered in staccato bursts as she moved between the sink and a narrow, old-fashioned stove.

"Did he know Robin Langley?"

"I don't know."

"Did you know Robin Langley?"

There was a brief flicker in her eyes when she answered. "I thought you came here to talk about Edward's accident."

"Now I'm asking about Miss Langley. Did you know her?"

"I'm sure you know that I did."

"What can you tell me about her?"

Without warning, her mood changed. "I don't know why you think an old woman like me would know anything about a pretty young girl from Memphis." She was smiling at him now, almost flirtatious.

Goodley returned her smile.

She turned away, took cups and saucers from a cupboard. "Take anything in your tea?" She moved a stack of catalogs, clearing a space before him on the table.

He shook his head. "We were talking about Robin Langley."

"You don't give up, do you?"

Goodley shook his head. "How did you know her?"

"Brad Wilson . . . I know you know who he is . . . brought her here, wanted to show her off."

"Your relationship with Brad Wilson?"

"A friend."

"Known him long?"

"Little over four years. That's how long he's lived in the cabin."

"You met him when he first moved in?"

"Yes. The cabin's on my property. It was just sitting there, full of dust and cobwebs and only the Good Lord knows what else. One day this skinny kid knocked on my door and asked if he could rent it. I told him I wasn't sure it was fit to live in. Not even a lock on the door. He laughed at that. Said he didn't have anything anybody'd want to steal. I told him if he wanted to give it a try, it was okay with me. A week or so later I went down there. Just to check. Couldn't believe my eyes when I saw how he'd cleaned it up."

"So he rents the cabin from you?"

"Yes. Well, actually, it's more like a trade. He lives there in exchange for helping me out around here. It's a good arrangement for both of us. He doesn't make that much money singing and playing that guitar of his, and there's things around here I can't do now that I'm getting older. And he's good company. Doesn't talk much. Lets me do things for him."

"What sort of things?"

"I made curtains for the cabin. Planted some flowers." She stopped, smiled sheepishly. "I know he don't give a tinker's damn about curtains and flowers, but it made me feel good to have somebody to do for, and he was nice enough to act like he was glad to have 'em."

"It must be hard. Living alone on a farm like this."

She shrugged. "I'm pretty independent. Maybe that's why me and Brad hit it off."

"The two of you are close?"

She looked at him and held up two fingers, touching each other along their entire length.

"You know where he came from? Anything about his background?"

"I know he's decent. Wouldn't kill anybody, if that's what you're asking."

"I didn't say that."

"No. But you're here. And I can pretty much imagine what those people said about him."

"Those people?"

"Robin's people."

"You ever met Robin's people?"

"No. Don't have to. Met plenty like 'em. Folks who don't get their hands dirty." The fey, flirtatious quality was gone now.

Goodley studied her before he said, "Tell me about your relationship with Robin Langley. How'd you meet her?"

Emma came over to the table and sat in the chair across from him. "Brad brought her here. Proud as a little boy with his first puppy."

"He loved her?"

"Oh, he loved her all right. It was enough to break your heart to see the way he looked at her."

"Did she love him?"

"Maybe some. Not enough."

"Enough for what?"

"To stand up to her father. That man thought Brad was the devil incarnate."

Goodley did not comment on this. He flipped through the papers on the clipboard. "Webster Barrons said he brought Miss Langley here once."

Emma nodded.

"Do you remember the circumstances?"

"Yes. It was a Saturday morning. She was real upset about something. They drove up. I was working outside. She asked if I knew where Brad was. I told her I didn't."

"Did you?"

"Know where he was?"

Goodley nodded.

Emma shrugged. "Don't remember. I might have." She met the policeman's eyes. "Yes, I would lie to keep her away from him." She sounded defiant, as though daring Goodley to disapprove.

"Why didn't you like her?"

"I didn't have anything against her, but she meant trouble for Brad. I could feel that in my bones."

"You said earlier she loved him, but not enough to stand up to her father. According to what I've heard"—he tapped the clipboard with his fingertips—"she did stand up to her father."

"For a while, sure. I meant for the long haul. I knew that boy was gonna get hurt."

"Why?"

"Different species."

"Excuse me?"

"You a gardener?"

"No."

"You take a flower . . . move it to a foreign environment. Never works. No matter how pretty it looks. One of two things happens. Either it withers and dies because it can't adapt, or it adapts too much and takes over, changes the environment 'til the plants there originally might as well be dead." Emma rose from the table and began striding around the kitchen. "I've seen it happen too many times"—she paused to pinch a faded bloom from an African violet—"to think this would be different."

Goodley didn't comment.

She stopped pacing and asked, "You about finished?"

"Just a couple more questions."

She sighed and sat down.

"Did you notice any change in the relationship between Brad Wilson and Miss Langley lately?"

"Such as?"

"Any mention of marriage plans?"

"Matter of fact, yes. Brad told me they planned to drive down to New Orleans and get married. I made it plain that I thought he was making a mistake. He got huffy and left."

"Did you happen to see him the morning of August twenty-eighth?"

"No."

"Do you know what he was doing that morning?"

"No."

He noted, but did not comment on, the clipped agressiveness of the second "no" and asked casually, "How about you? Do you remember what you were doing that morning?"

"I can't say I remember, but I was probably working out in the yard. That's how I spend most mornings. Why? Am I a suspect, Lieutenant?"

"Just a routine question. I ask that of everyone."

"I see. Anything else you want from me?"

"How well do you know the Connorses?"

"Not at all. Well, I did meet her. Just this morning. She was poking around Barney's, asking questions."

"What kind of questions?"

Emma grinned. "Same kind of questions you're asking."

"Back to the morning Webster Barrons brought Miss Langley here. Did you ever find out why she was so upset?"

"No."

"Weren't you curious? Since you're so close to Wilson and she was looking for him?"

She shrugged.

"You didn't ask what was wrong?"

"I've been around long enough to know that people, especially young people, don't tell you things because you ask. They tell you when they're ready. You should know that."

Goodley smiled.

"I'll say this, though. It had something to do with her death."

"What makes you think that?"

"Nothing I can put my finger on." She shook her head. "These old bones again."

"You must have some reason."

"No. I've told you everything I can. Now I've got work to do." And she picked up the gardening gloves and left him sitting at the table with his lukewarm tea.

Chapter Eighteen

*T*hree weeks now—and they still don't know who killed her. Eyes wide, Jennie stared into the dark, trying to sort out everything that had happened since the day her car was stolen. Tom and Robin. She squeezed her eyes shut, fighting the sick rage that swept through her when she thought of the two of them together. *Stop. Have to think of Tommy and Andy. What's best for them? I know he loves them. Loves me too. The way his eyes follow me. Doesn't matter. Just gives him a stronger motive. But he'd never put the body in our car. Or hide the jack behind our house. Kids play there all the time. Tom couldn't be that stupid. What if he was desperate? The kids. Their father can't be a murderer. What if he is?* She rolled over on the couch and pounded her fist into the pillow, trying to get comfortable. *I'll deal with it. But I have to know.*

She forced her thoughts away from Tom. *Brad.* She wondered if Brad knew about Tom and Robin. That would certainly give him a motive. *And he might put the body in our car to get back at Tom.* Unbidden, the image of the small hand came to mind. She pictured the hand moving along the familiar contours of Tom's body and hated herself for caring more that Robin had been with Tom than that the poor girl was dead. Tom. Brad. Who else? Web? What if Robin wanted to break up and he didn't? *Wish I knew what happened there.* She shook her head. *Somehow, I just don't see him that passionate about anything. Guess I shouldn't count him out. Somehow, I have to find out more about both of them—Brad and Web. Tom? Please, God, no.*

Giving up on sleep, exhausted by her doubts, she switched on the lamp and tried to read. Unsuccessfully. Compared to her own tangled life, the intricate plot seemed bland. It didn't matter. The book was mostly for the benefit of the kids, should they discover her on the couch and wonder why she wasn't in bed with their father. *Bed with Tom. Something else to deal with. Not yet. When this murder thing is cleared up. Kids don't need another disruption in their lives right now.*

Relieved when light broke through the slats of the wooden blinds, she got up and started coffee. Still needing something to do, she chopped pecans and made batter for waffles.

"Why can't we have cereal? Like always?" Andy demanded later as they waited for the waffle iron to heat.

"We don't always have cereal for breakfast," she said.

Tommy broke in, "We usually just have waffles on Sunday. School days we're s'posed to have cereal and fruit."

Tom said, "Hey, guys, Mom made us a treat. Don't give her a hard time." He looked at Jennie, obviously hoping for some show of gratitude.

She sent back a wordless but unmistakable message: *Forget it, slimebag.*

The give-and-take over breakfast, getting Tom off to work and the kids to the bus stop, pushed other concerns to the back of her mind. After that, alone and with time on her hands, the doubts and questions crept back. Laundry seemed as good a distraction as any, so she began the routine of sorting by color and emptying pockets. As usual, the smallest jeans, Andy's, yielded the biggest pile. She was careful not to throw away any treasures. She had learned, but would never understand, how much a small boy could value apparently useless items, such as rocks and bits of string. She saved even the dead beetle, using a finger and a thumb to lift it by one wirelike leg. Tommy's pile was next. Not so much from him: two purple jelly beans and a sticky, folded-over piece of paper, surely not worth saving. Her hand was suspended over the wastebasket when, deciding to play it safe, she unfolded the paper. It turned out to be the discarded backing from a Polaroid picture. *Jeez! Didn't know anybody used these things anymore.* Curious, she turned the cardboard square until the light hit it just right and she could make out the image of two small figures—Tommy and Andy, she guessed, not that she could really tell. She put the sticky square next to the beetle, wondering who had taken the picture, and, more important, why.

The chugging of the washing machine blended with the hum of the refrigerator and Smokey's deep purr. Lulled by the intimacy of mundane sound, she picked up the two-day-old newspaper where she'd marked the account of Pynchon's accident. Her shoulders hunched in concentration as she read the article for the umpteenth time.

"Thank God they didn't mention my name," she said aloud. There was, in fact, nothing to connect the accident to the murder. "I guess that's a good sign," she muttered as she folded the paper to fit into her tote bag and went to get a map from the desk.

An hour and a half later, she pulled into Riverview Manor's parking lot. She eased past an ambulance and a police car and found a space at the end of the building.

Riverview's East Wing was reserved for residents whose declining health required nursing care. There was always a feeling of controlled chaos about that section in the mornings until everyone was bathed or showered, the beds changed, and laundry collected. Today, however, though the activity was markedly less, the feeling of control was missing. The nurses at the desk in the center of the lobby appeared distracted as they shuffled papers around the cluttered surface. Myrna Friedman, the financial administrator, was hurrying along the corridor, mumbling under her breath. Jennie caught a few words—something about bureaucrats and improper jurisdiction.

Melinda, a high school student who worked a few hours in the mornings to earn college credit, came hurrying through the swinging doors leading from the East Wing. "The patient they just brought in has a police guard," she said in a conspiratorial whisper. Before she could say any more, Mrs. Friedman came back, now accompanied by the head nurse.

The nurse stopped to scold Melinda. "This is no time to gossip."

"Yes, ma'am." The freckle-faced teenager scuttled away.

Jennie exchanged glances with an aide pushing an elderly man in a wheelchair.

"Maybe there was a shooting," the old man said. "Lots of crime these days."

Jennie said, "Wouldn't a shooting victim be in a regular hospital?" She went to the door leading to the East Wing, where she stood to one side and peered through the small, square window at the top of the door. She watched through narrowed eyes, straining to see the figure on the gurney being wheeled into Room E46. A nurse in crisp whites stepped sideways, keeping pace and holding aloft a shapeless, clear bag connected to the supine figure by plastic tubes. In the hall just outside E46, a uniformed policeman was listening respectfully to a man whose face Jennie could not see. But even with his back to her, there was no mistaking that tall, spare figure. She watched an aide bring a plastic chair and place it just outside the door. She quickly stepped back when Goodley turned around.

"I bet," she said under her breath, "it's Mr. Pynchon." A quick glance at her watch told her she'd have to postpone checking the admissions office until after the morning sing-along.

When she entered the activities room, she forced a brightness to her voice that she did not feel. "Good morning, everyone." For an hour and a half she played the piano and sang along with residents, choosing songs that reminded them of their youth, ending, as always, with "God Bless America"; the fervor with which they sang this particular song brought tears to her eyes.

"Okay, that's it for today," she said as soon as the voices faded. She wrinkled her nose and added, "My guess is you're having macaroni and cheese for lunch." Nods and smiles agreed with her.

In a hurry to get to the admissions office before it closed at noon, she cut short her usual chats, promising herself she'd make it up to them. But despite her efforts, when she arrived at the office door, she was greeted by a neatly lettered sign:

CLOSED FOR THE DAY
IN CASE OF EMERGENCY, SEE NURSING SUPERVISOR

Oh, well. Other things to think about right now anyway.

She seated herself on a couch in the nearly deserted lounge, took the map and newspaper out of her tote bag, and lay them on the coffee table before her. When a dark shape appeared on the surface of her papers, she was not surprised to see it was Goodley who cast the shadow.

"Mind if I sit down?"

Surprised that he bothered to ask, she shook her head.

"Know why I'm here?"

"Let me guess. That's Mr. Pynchon in E46, isn't it?"

He nodded.

"Why here? And why the police guard? Seems a bit much for an accident victim."

"Just a precaution."

"Does the fact that he had a card with my name in his pocket have anything to do with it?"

"I don't believe in coincidence, Mrs. Connors."

She hated the way he looked into her eyes, as though he were reading her thoughts. She looked down and remembered her purpose in bringing the map. "Will you show me exactly where he had the accident? I'm not all that familiar with the back roads in River County."

He pointed to a narrow line on the map. "That's Gray Mule Road"—he moved his finger along the line to where it took a sharp turn—"and this is where his car left the road and struck a tree."

"That's almost a forty-five-degree angle. I should think there'd be a lot of accidents there."

Goodley moved his finger a fraction of an inch. "This is where he lives."

Jennie studied the map. "In other words, he was practically in his own backyard. So he knew the road."

The policeman nodded and leaned over the map again. "Here's Barnstable's Flea Market. And here's where you found your car with Miss Langley's body."

Jennie drew a mental triangle connecting Barney's, the accident scene, and the spot where she'd discovered Robin. *They're all so close.* She felt Goodley watching her. *He thinks there's a connection. That's why he's being so nice. He hopes I'll let down my guard and spill the beans.*

"Come with me," he said abruptly, rising from the couch so quickly that his knee banged the coffee table.

"Where?"

"We're going to see Mr. Pynchon."

"Can we do that?"

He did not answer immediately. When they were walking down the hall together he said, "He's conscious, but he hasn't spoken."

"You mean he can't speak?"

"The doctors aren't sure about that."

When they went through the swinging doors to the East Wing, Jennie saw two people standing in front of E46 talking to the policemen. The woman had a huge bouquet of rust-colored chrysanthemums in her arms. Jennie recognized Emma from the flea market. The second person was Brad Wilson. *What's he doing here?* She looked at Goodley to see if he shared her surprise. As usual, his poker face revealed nothing. He did, however, quicken his pace so that Jennie had to take little skipping steps to keep up.

When Emma saw Jennie and Goodley approaching, she left the side of the young policeman and came toward them.

"No visitors," Goodley said before she had a chance to speak. He reached for the flowers. "I'll be glad to give these to him."

"You mean it's okay for the police to harass him, but not for his old friends to visit," Emma said.

"I don't intend to harass him," Goodley said. "I'm here for his protection."

"From what?" Emma snapped. She pointed to Jennie when Goodley didn't answer. "What about her?"

Goodley's tone revealed no emotion. "Do you want to leave the flowers?"

Emma looked disgusted, but she relinquished the bouquet and left without further comment. Brad, who had observed the scene in silence, followed.

Goodley turned to the policeman and said, "You can break for lunch now. I'll take over until you come back." When the young man had gone, he said to Jennie, "Ready?"

She hesitated. "Are you sure it's okay? You just told them"—she tilted her head in the direction Brad and Emma had gone—"no visitors."

"It's okay if I say it is."

It took Jennie a minute to recognize the figure on the bed. She had seen Edward Pynchon only once before and under very different circumstances. There was no doubt, however, that he recognized her. He moved his lips, but there was no sound. He held his hand out to her.

She stepped closer, afraid he might dislodge the needle taped to his arm.

Goodley moved in behind her.

The old man looked up, seemed to see Goodley for the first time. He looked back at Jennie momentarily as though sending her a message, and then closed his eyes. The lines on the machine by the bed began to flutter. Alarmed, Jennie pressed the buzzer lying next to his pillow.

A nurse appeared instantly. She stopped when she saw Jennie and Goodley. "What's going on in here?" She entered the room, glanced at the machine. "Out!"

Chapter Nineteen

Three hours later, Jennie was sitting in her kitchen telling Kate about the incident. "He wanted to tell me something, but when he saw Goodley, he clammed up. Pretended to fall asleep."

"At least now you know you're right," Kate said. "Goodley believes there's a connection between Robin and Pynchon."

"And the connection must be Brad."

Kate said, "Why do you suppose he's in Riverview instead of a hospital up in River County?"

"I figure Goodley pulled some strings. You know how the Memphis police seem to be working hand in glove with him on this . . . he wants Pynchon here. If he's at Riverview, Goodley can watch him and keep an eye on me at the same time."

"Jennie, stop! Just give it a rest. He doesn't think you killed Robin. How could he?"

"How could he not?"

"But what about a motive? You said yourself—"

"I figure that's the only reason I'm not in jail right now. If he figures out any possible motive for me . . . I don't even want to think about that. I have to find the real killer first."

"First? Before what? He's not going to find a motive. You don't have one."

Jennie avoided commenting on this. Instead, she asked, "What would you think if you were in his shoes? Somebody reports a stolen car, and then shows up saying, 'Don't worry about my car. I found it. And, oh, by the way, there just happens to be a body in the backseat.' "

"At least you've regained your sense of humor. Thank God. I was getting worried."

"That bad, huh?"

Kate nodded. "This past week . . . you've been downright bitchy. Especially to Tom. Even Frank noticed. Said he'd never seen you like that. And poor Tom—what's wrong?"

Don't "Poor Tom" me! Without answering, she removed the cups from the table and set them in the sink with a ferocity that threatened to send shards of glass flying.

"Looks like I just hit a nerve."

"Drop it."

"Sure. But I take back what I said about your sense of humor."

Jennie kept her back to Kate, not trusting her face to keep the secret she was not ready to share, not even with her best friend.

"Hey, I was kidding."

Jennie maintained her silence and took a deep breath to compose herself.

"Sorry. Bad joke."

I'll get through this. With that thought firmly in mind, she turned to face Kate. "Let's forget it. Okay?" When Kate nodded, she said, "Remember the other day . . . when we were on our way to Barney's and I said I wanted to visit that bar, Southern Lites, some night when Brad was working?"

Kate nodded.

"The schedule had him listed for Wednesday."

Another nod, more cautious than the first.

"Well, how about it? Wanna go?"

"You mean this Wednesday? Tomorrow?"

"Gee, you catch on quick."

"I can't. Frank's working practically round the clock on a big job and there's no one to watch the kids." When Jennie didn't answer, she added, "Maybe next Wednesday."

"I have to go now. The sooner the better."

"Any chance Tom would go with you? Tell your parents you need a night out. They'll—"

"No. No. No. NO!"

They were interrupted by the sound of the kids' voices outside. Kate went to the door and called out, "Amelia. Trevor. I'm over here."

The four children came clattering in, Andy first. "Mom!" He stopped short, and then did a twirling half circle, his face twisted by disbelief when he saw the folded clothes stacked on an empty chair. "You didn't wash my pants from yesterday, did you?"

"I sure did."

"Oh, no," he wailed. "I found this great bug. I wanted to show Trevor."

"Hold on." She led him into the adjoining laundry room. "No reason to panic." She pointed to the two piles at the end of the sorting table. "Any of this look familiar?"

The other kids followed and watched Andy retrieve his prize. He held it up for all to admire.

"Oh, sick." Amelia turned away in disgust.

Delighted, Trevor and Tommy began to laugh.

Andy didn't see the humor; he was indignant. "It's not sick."

Experience had taught both mothers this was harmless, and they didn't get involved. Jennie saw Tommy pick up the Polaroid backing and asked, "Is that from a picture of you and Andy?"

"Yeah."

"Do you have the original?"

"Uh-uh."

"Looks like it might have been a pretty good picture."

He held the paper up for her closer inspection. "Andy only comes up to my shoulder."

She knew better than to comment on that. "Who took the picture?"

"One of the construction guys by the bus stop."

Alarmed, she asked, "Why did he take a picture of you?"

"He had this funny old-fashioned camera. He wanted to show his buddies how it works."

"Did he take pictures of all the kids?"

"No, just me and Andy."

She fought to keep panic at bay. "Why you two?"

The argument about the bug exhausted, Andy added his bit. "He likes us, Mom."

"What do you mean, he likes you?"

"He always talks to us."

"What does he say?"

"Nothing special. He just shows us his tools and stuff."

"Has he ever offered to give you anything? Take you anywhere?"

"No, Mom." Tommy's look at the ceiling said much more than the two simple words he spoke.

Andy patted her hand. "Don't worry, Mom, we know all about strangers."

"Don't forget."

They nodded at her, their faces mock serious in the universal manner of children humoring grown-up fears.

"We haven't had our snack yet," Tommy reminded her.

She got apple juice out of the refrigerator and peanut butter crackers from the cupboard before she tackled the issue at hand. "I mean it," she said, as she set a napkin and a glass in front of each child and poured apple juice while they helped themselves to the crackers. "Everything Daddy and I've told you about strangers is especially important to remember now."

There was a moment of ominous quiet, which Tommy broke. "Because of what happened to Robin?"

She nodded.

Still quiet, Andy took a sip of juice and looked from his mother to his brother.

No six-year-old face should look like that. She wanted to hold him and tell him not to worry. Instead she said in her sternest voice, "That man at the construction site . . . He's a stranger. Even if you see him every day, he's still a stranger. Don't forget that."

Kate looked at Trevor and Amelia. "You guys, too. Listen to what Jennie's saying."

They nodded back at her. More serious faces.

"There's no real reason to think there's a connection between that guy and the murder," Kate pointed out later, as they sat at the table tucked into the bay of the kitchen window.

"You have to admit, though, the situation's weird. Something's definitely off-kilter."

Kate did not disagree and, for the moment, Jennie didn't press the matter. They looked toward the scene outside, where their children ran back and forth across the yard in pursuit of a soccer ball. From the sunlit open area into the shadows cast by the oak tree, the lithe, small bodies moved as effortlessly and tirelessly as ripples on the surface of a lake. Jennie watched, spellbound by their grace, terrified by their vulnerability.

Kate broke the silence. "Don't go to that bar. Not by yourself."

"I'll be perfectly safe."

"There's no such thing as perfectly safe."

Chapter Twenty

Jennie slowed when she approached the school. Morning recess time. She looked for her kids and saw Andy immediately, a study in the joy of motion, legs pumping, arms stretched wide, head thrown back. He turned, as though to say something to another boy, and continued to move backward without lessening his pace. She held her breath when he almost ran into the slide, and breathed again when he stopped in time.

Just past the playground, she came to the parking lot, and caught her breath again. A green truck with a shell on the back was parked near the driveway. Going at a snail's pace now, she looked in the rearview mirror; a man with a bandanna tied around his head was leaning against a tree watching the children. She followed his gaze to a trio of boys near the base of the slide. There was no doubt he was focused on Andy. *Who is he? Does anyone know he's here?* She intended to find out.

Half an hour later, after a lively discussion with the principal, she returned to her car, only partially reassured by her guarantee that anyone working on school property was carefully checked by the proper authorities and that workmen never came into the building, not even to use the restrooms; they had their own portable toilets outside. And, yes, the principal had assured her, a staff member always watched as the children boarded the buses. They were extremely careful in these matters. *You darn well better be!*

She waited until halfway through dinner to tell them. "I'm going to a movie tonight." She kept her tone casual, hoping to slip the announcement by with a minimum of fuss. No such luck.

113

Tom stopped with his knife poised over the butter dish and glanced at the children before he looked across the table to Jennie.

"By myself," she added, lifting her chin.

Peas tumbled off Andy's fork. "Mom," he said, "you can't go to a movie by yourself."

"Sure I can."

"Well, you never did before." Tommy spoke as though that settled the matter.

She silenced him by kissing her index finger and placing it on his lips as she said, "Cookies for dessert in case anybody's interested. Chocolate chippers."

The boys were more interested in the cookies than their mother's night out. Tom, on the other hand, had that look, but Jennie didn't care. In fact, she reveled in it.

Later, when she stuffed a flashlight into her oversized purse, he didn't ask for an explanation, but she felt compelled to give one. Old habits die hard. "If I have a flat tire or something . . . those things never happen when you're close to a service station." She realized she was overexplaining and finished with a shrug. She kissed both boys good-bye and, since they were watching, gave their father a quick peck on the cheek before she left.

As she backed the rental car out of the garage, Kate came running across the narrow strip of lawn separating the two driveways. "You really going through with it?" she asked. "All by yourself?"

"Honestly, Kate. Not you too."

"What'd you tell Tom?"

"That I was going to a movie."

"Alone?"

"Uh-huh."

"He didn't object?"

"I didn't ask permission." Jennie studied her best friend's face. She looked as shocked as the boys had been. *Am I really that predictable? I'm going to have to start surprising people more often.*

"I thought I knew you," Kate said, "but this, going out there all alone." She shook her head. "You have your phone with you?"

Jennie often didn't take her phone, mostly because she refused to be one of the legion of users who seemed oblivious to the intrusions they created. Tonight, however, one might come in handy. By way of answer, she pulled the phone and the flashlight out of her purse for Kate to see. "Wish me luck," she said, tossing both devices on the seat beside her.

"Forget about luck! Be careful. Call me when you get home. Okay?"

"There's nothing to worry about," Jennie assured her. "It's a public place."

"Call. No matter how late."

Jennie laughed, gaining confidence from her friend's concern.

That must be Southern Lites, she thought, when she saw the multicolored neon fireworks surrounding a giant sl against the sky. She was so intent on looking at the sign she forgot the turn indicator. *Oops, sorry about that.* She looked in the rearview mirror and apologized mentally to the driver behind her, an egg-shaped outline in the rectangle of her vehicle's mirror. Postponing the moment when she must walk into the roadhouse alone, she sat in her car and watched the other vehicle, a pickup truck with a shell on the back, drive past. She remembered the truck in the school parking lot this morning and wondered if it could be the same. The silhouette was the same. It was too dark to distinguish the color. She watched the vehicle pass Southern Lites and turn into a driveway a little farther down the road. Curious, she continued to watch, noting that it stopped just after turning in, though the lights of the farmhouse were set back another hundred yards or more. *What's he waiting for? Whatever it is, I can't sit here worrying about it. One thing at a time,* she told herself and got out of the car.

She opened the door, took a few steps into the smoky interior, and then stopped, taken aback by a snarling bobcat head mounted on the wall.

"Evening." The man behind the bar smiled. "You lost? Need some directions?"

"No. I'd like a drink."

"Name your poison."

"I'll have a Diet Coke," she said, moving forward when the door behind her opened. She knew she should have a beer, but alcohol made her sleepy, and she needed to be sharp this evening. "Guess that's not too poisonous." She laughed, she hoped casually, and took another step forward so the man who had just come in the door could get by.

"Excuse me," he said and eased past her. He nodded, but did not meet her eyes. He was bald, his head the same egg-shape as the driver of the truck.

"Here you are." The bartender—zac was embroidered on his shirt pocket—placed the red and white can on the bar along with a glass. "Sheila," he said in a slightly louder voice. A middle-aged woman with very curly hair, highly blushed cheeks, and improbable eyelashes looked their way. "Why don't you help this little lady find a nice table?"

"Sure. Follow me, honey." She led Jennie into the other room and stopped at a table near where the microphone was set up.

"Could I sit over there?" Jennie pointed to a table in the far corner.

"Anywhere you like. Plenty of room tonight. Especially back there. Most people like to sit closer to the stage."

"When does it start? The entertainment, I mean."

Sheila glanced at her watch. "About fifteen minutes." She watched Jennie select the chair farthest from the light and asked, "Somebody gonna be meetin' you?"

"No. I'm on my own." She took a perverse pleasure in the woman's apparent belief that she was involved in an illicit rendezvous. *That's what I should do. Sauce for the goose.*

She sipped her Coke and, as her eyes adjusted to the dimmer lighting in this room, looked around, noticing that about half the tables were occupied, mostly by couples. They all greeted each other like old friends. *Good,* she thought when she saw the spotlight directed toward the stage. *The light'll shine in Brad's eyes and he won't see me back here.* The bald man who had come in after Jennie came to the door. He squinted and looked around the room. Jennie thought his eyes lingered on her a few seconds too long. She tried to remember how long the vehicle had been behind her. She pushed the idea away. *I'm getting paranoid.* But it kept coming back. She thought of the man with the bandanna on the playground. *Who? And why?* Questions ran through her head like mice through a maze.

They were put aside when the spotlight went on. This is what she'd come for—to learn more about Brad Wilson. Did he have another girlfriend? Someone who might want to get rid of Robin? Or—she didn't really know what she was looking for, but trusted her instincts to recognize it when (and if) it appeared.

Brad walked to the tall stool in the center of the stage, sat down, and without speaking, began to play his guitar. He was dressed in jeans, a close-fitting denim shirt, and western boots. Except for an ornate silver belt, his attire was low-key, its plainness accentuating the wiry tautness of his body. Cradling the twelve-string in his arms as though it were a much-loved child, he appeared more at ease than she had ever seen him. Watching him, listening to him, she understood why Robin had been attracted.

She turned her attention to the other people in the room. More tables had filled during the last few minutes. The crowd was still mostly couples. At the table nearest the stage, however, there was a young woman with long, dark red hair. She was alone the only woman except Jennie who was. The redhead watched Brad with rapt attention, moving her body suggestively with the beat. As far as Jennie could tell, Brad was completely immersed in his music. She was trying to determine if he was aware of the girl when Sheila set another Coke in front of her. Surprised, Jennie said, "I didn't—"

"Compliments of that gentleman over there," Sheila told her, pointing to a man with dark hair, slicked straight back from his forehead. His too-tight cowboy shirt strained over a rounded belly.

"But—"

"He told me to give you another of whatever you're drinking," Sheila said. She winked at Jennie. "I didn't tell him what it was," she added, then moved away, threading her way through the tables.

The man with the slicked-back hair came over and stood between Jennie and the spotlighted area. "Mind if I sit down?"

"Actually, yes. I do mind."

"Oh, come on. Doesn't seem right. Pretty little thing like you. Sitting here all by yourself."

Jennie gave him a brief, dismissive glance, and then moved her chair so she could see past him.

"Feisty too. I like that."

Several people at the edge of the crowd shifted slightly and glanced her way. One man turned around and was watching, an amused look on his face.

"Name's George," the intruder said, pulling a chair closer before he sat down.

She could smell the pomade on his greasy, obviously dyed hair. *This guy's not going to give up easy,* she thought. *I'll have to be as rude as he is. Oh, well, good manners weren't meant for such as he.* Two more people had turned around. *I can't make a scene, though. I don't want Brad to know I'm here.*

Restraining all the things she wanted to say to the creep, she picked up her purse and headed toward the door marked REST-ROOMS.

She heard Brad's voice as she walked along the short hall where the restrooms were located. "Here's one you all know before I take a short break." She turned and hurried back to the door leading into the main room, wanting to see if Brad joined the redhead when the set was over. She looked toward the table in the corner. George was still there, his arm resting cozily on the back of her chair. *I'll sit at another table. That might discourage him. No. Not him. There's no way to get rid of him without calling attention to myself.* She was standing in the shadow, trying to figure out her next move when Sheila came through the door and collided with her.

"Sorry about that, honey. You okay?"

"I'm fine. You?"

"Oh, I'm fine. Takes more than a little bump to hurt an old bird like me. I'd move though, if I were you. It's almost break time. Every woman in the place's gonna head for the ladies. If you stay here, you'll get trampled."

Jennie attempted a laugh. "I was checking out the situation be-fore I went back."

Sheila glanced over her shoulder. "You mean George?" she said. "No use waiting for him to leave. He's our local ladies' man; thinks 'no' means 'I just love hearin' you ask.'"

"I was ready to leave anyway," Jennie lied.

"Be careful. He's so sure he's irresistible he's not above following you to your car."

Jennie remembered Sheila's sly wink when she delivered the Diet Coke and knew she had an ally. She wasn't really worried about George, but didn't want the bald man to see her leave. For some reason, he made her nervous. "I don't suppose there's a back door I could use."

Sheila winked again and motioned for Jennie to follow her. They went down the hall, past the restrooms, and through a door marked PRIVATE. The room they stepped into was obviously part of someone's living quarters, a strong contrast to the dark, polished oak of the public area. Ruffles and bows abounded. On the wall over the sofa was a needleworked version of the SL sign, complete with surrounding wavy lines in fiery colors. Jennie could feel Sheila's eyes on her face and knew a comment was expected.

"Did you make that?" she asked, indicating the needlework.

Sheila nodded proudly.

"It's really nice," Jennie said, bending forward to admire the thousands of tiny stitches. It was nice. The design was gaudy, but the workmanship was beautiful.

Sheila acknowledged the compliment with a nod, said, "Well, I have to get back. The bathrooms aren't the only things that get rushed at breaktime." She led Jennie through to the kitchen, unlocked the back door, and stood aside as she stepped out into the night. "You can circle around the building either way, and you'll be right back in the parking lot. Be careful. It's real dark out there."

Outside, Jennie looked up at the sky. The thin sliver of a moon was cut in half by one of the wispy clouds floating above the treetops; its light was not enough to relieve the almost total darkness. She could feel rather than see the nearness of the forest. An early cold front had passed through in the afternoon, leaving it unusually cool for mid-September. A slight wind began to blow, causing the dried leaves to whisper, repeating Sheila's parting words: *Be careful.*

She moved slowly, keeping one hand on the building to guide her over the unfamiliar terrain until she came to the corner. Along the side of the building, the light from the windows cast yellow squares onto the black earth, creating a grid, reminding her of the playing board of a huge game. She picked her way carefully to the first bright square and stopped at its edge.

Maybe George was a blessing in disguise. She peered through the uncurtained window and looked toward the table in the back corner. Apparently he had given up. That corner of the room was deserted except for a few people milling about and talking in front of the RESTROOMS sign. On the stage Brad's guitar leaned against the stool; the spotlight had been turned off. There was Brad—next to the red-head. Her hand was on his arm and she stood so close to him that she had to tilt her head back to look into his face. She was laughing, showing off perfect teeth.

Brad's back was to the window so Jennie couldn't judge his reaction. *Turn around,* she willed. To no avail. She tried to read his posture. Impossible. He kept his hands at his sides until someone put a beer in one of them. He did not, however, move away from the redhead. *What a jerk!*

She looked around, wondering if she would recognize anyone else in the crowd. She saw the egg-shaped head, swiveling as though looking for someone. *Time to go.* The night air cut through her light jacket. *A few more minutes,* she thought, hoping Brad would turn around so she could see his face, but he did not. The redhead stayed at his side, clinging to his arm. The bald man moved through the room, heading toward the restrooms. There was no longer any doubt in her mind who he was looking for. *I have to get out of here.*

Back at the car, she began the usual rummaging for keys. "How do they always manage to work their way to the bottom?" she muttered. When she finally found the keys, she looked toward Southern Lites' entrance. The door remained safely closed. She was alone in the parking lot. So far, so good.

She fiddled with the radio while she waited for an oncoming car to pass. She looked around the parking lot again, saw the truck with the shell, and smiled. The car passed, leaving the road home clear. But Jennie turned the other way, her smile broadening. After her success in evading George and Baldy, she felt invincible.

Chapter Twenty-one

The moon disappeared behind a cloud, leaving only the head-lights to carve a path. A male voice whined from the radio, crying over a love gone wrong. "Tell me about it," Jennie said, and punched a button to cut short the lament. The radio's response was a female voice. Equally sorrowful. Another button   organ music, more plain tive than both. A quick twist of a dial—and lonely silence.

She reached for the phone on the seat beside her, pushed in the numbers for something a little more friendly, listened to the ring, and smiled when she heard Kate's anxious, "Hello?"

"Hi, it's me."

"Jennie! Thank God!"

"You must have been right by the phone."

"I haven't budged all night. How'd it go?"

"It was . . . interesting."

"What's that mean?"

"I'll tell you tomorrow."

"Okay. Anyway, I'm glad you're home."

"Actually, I'm not home. I'm calling from the car."

"Have you called Tom?"

"No. Why should I?"

"He called here right after you left. Wanted to know if I knew what movie you were going to."

"What'd you tell him?"

"That I didn't know."

"What'd he say?"

"Not much. He seemed . . . I don't know . . . strange."

No comment from Jennie.

"Jen—"

"Yeah?"

"Call him. Let him know you're okay."

"Maybe."

She held the phone a few minutes after she said good-bye to Kate, and then tossed it on the seat. "Let him worry," she said aloud.

When she came to Brad's cabin, she stopped the car and watched the line of clouds move on, exposing the thin moon. *Okay, you're here. What next?* The road ahead glowed dully, a leaden stream between banks of towering pine trees. It stretched straight for about fifty yards, and then was lost to view. She drove toward the spot where the road seemed to disappear. Just beyond the curve, she looked in the rearview mirror, nodded, pulled over to the side, and stopped. From here, the car would not be seen by anyone going only as far as Brad's house. A few feet ahead the road ended. She reached for the bulky purse, changed her mind. *I'll leave it here. It's safe.* She removed the keys, slipped them in her pocket, put the purse on the floor of the car and picked up the flashlight.

She kept her thumb on the switch but did not turn the light on; the scant rays of the moon and the sound produced by her shoes crunching on the gravel were enough to keep her from straying off the road. When she came to the house, she made her way up the steps, past the wood stacked neatly at the front edge of the porch, and went to the window.

She turned on the flashlight and looked inside, telling her conscience to mind its own business. The beam fell first on a chair, a high-backed rocker that cast a ladderlike shadow on the shelves that lined the back wall. She looked past the chair and examined the contents of the shelves: books, records, stereo equipment. She moved the beam of light to the left wall of the room: an old-fashioned, round-topped refrigerator; a sink mounted on the wall below a window; next to the sink, a wooden cabinet; over the cabinet, open shelves, filled with a few dishes, some pots, pans; an iron skillet hanging on a nail; a wood stove of the type used for both cooking and heating. The opposite wall had a single cot-type bed pushed into the corner. At the foot of the bed was a wooden table with two chairs tilted against one edge. She nodded in approval of the Spartan tidiness and turned the light back to the center of the room. A garment was draped over the back of the rocking chair. She focused on the article of clothing.

A bright flash caught her eye. *Headlights?* She looked up the road. *Yes.* She turned off her flashlight. *Brad? Not yet. Too early.* She thought of the bald man, shook her head, confident he could not have followed her. She stepped back from the window and crouched behind the woodpile. The lights grew larger, bouncing crazily on the uneven road. *That must be Brad. I can't get to the car without being seen. Maybe I can slip off the porch and hide against the side of the house until he's inside.* Alert, but not actually afraid, she crouched lower, prepared to crawl to the edge of the porch. *Whoever it is, they're coming here. There's nowhere else to go. Maybe it's not Brad. Who else could it be? The redhead? Is she coming here to wait for him? Could be. I have to know.*

She moved closer to the stacked wood and pulled her jacket up so the collar covered most of her face but did not obstruct her view of the steps or the door. The lights were brighter now. They bounced and made a wide arc, changing direction as the vehicle pulled into the parking area beside the house. A tarpaulin was draped loosely over the end of the woodpile; she hid behind this and waited, listening for the opening car door. Would there be one passenger or two? Had Brad brought the redhead home with him? But there was only the sound of the engine. Slowly and cautiously, she raised a corner of the tarp and looked toward the driveway. *Not Brad! Not his van. Not the pickup truck either. Thank God for that! But who?*

She narrowed her eyes and tried to see into the car. No luck. Darkness rendered the driver invisible. She concentrated on the profile of the vehicle. It was a fairly late model sedan. She didn't know what kind; there was nothing distinctive about it. The color? In this light she couldn't tell—something dark. Then, without ever having turned off the engine or the headlights, the vehicle backed out and headed down the dead-end road. *My car! They'll find my car! Is that what they're looking for? Why?* By the time she thought to look at the license plate, the car was too far away for her to read the number.

The area between the house and the car was mostly pines, with tall, slender trunks reaching toward the sky, leaving the forest floor to scrubby, low-growing thicket. She watched through the trees as the car's headlights hit the back of her rental car. The distance was less than she had thought. She remembered how the road curved back on itself. The vehicle's headlights disappeared abruptly. She assumed they had been turned off.

From her vantage point on the porch, she could see over most of the underbrush, with only the thin lines of the tree trunks and an occasional tangle of vine to obstruct her view. While she watched, the car door opened and a bulky figure stepped out. The clouds were gone now and Jennie could see the figure moving toward her car. She watched as a flashlight beam was directed through her car's window. Then the door of her car opened and the interior light went on, outlining the shadowy figure. She remembered her purse, put her hand in her pocket and felt the comforting solidity of the keys resting there. *If he turns around now, I'll have a good look at his face,* she thought. But the car door closed, extinguishing the light, before the intruder turned around. In the almost total darkness, Jennie could detect movement, but nothing else. She heard a muffled thud, but had no idea what it was. Again, when the door to the sedan was opened, she strained for a better look, but the face and figure of the driver remained a silhouette, half merged with the trees and vines of the forest. The sedan turned around and headed back up the road toward the cabin. Jennie lay flat on the floor of the porch, as close to the woodpile as she could get.

She heard the car pass by without stopping. Pressed against the wood pile, she raised herself cautiously from her hiding place and tried again to make out a license number, but the car bumping up and down on the rough road made this impossible. Then, still curious about the garment hanging from the chair, she returned to the window and trained the beam of light for another look. *It's too small to be Brad's. It belongs to a woman.* She shone the light around other areas of the one-room house, looking for more evidence of a female presence. The ruffled curtains at the window over the sink caught her attention.

The wind was blowing harder now, moving across the tops of the pines, a lonely sound. She shivered and pulled her jacket closer. *I wonder how late he works. Maybe the redhead will come home with him. I could hide somewhere and wait for them.* She looked at the luminous dial of her watch: a little after ten. *How much longer?* she wondered. *What if he went home with the redhead? I'll wait outside Southern Lites and watch him leave. That should tell me something. But where can I wait? What will I do with the car?* She thought briefly of Tom, knew he must be wondering why she wasn't home yet, and shrugged the thought away. *I can't go now,* she thought, *the whole thing's wasted effort if I don't find out about Brad and the redhead.*

She tried to remember the exact layout of the area around Southern Lites as she put the tarp back in place and started toward the steps. Passing the door, some impulse made her try the knob. She froze momentarily as it turned in her hand. Without allowing herself to think about consequences, she opened it and entered the house.

She went directly to the rocking chair, planning to hold the sleeve of the shirt (or blouse) up to her arm to determine the size. A gong seemed to sound at that moment. She grabbed at the rocker, the only tangible thing within reach. The ladderlike shadow on the wall became a living thing and began to jump up and down in fury. She turned off her flashlight and the demon vanished. She exhaled in relief and took a slow step backward, wondering what had set off echoes in the stillness. She turned the light back on and directed its beam toward the floor. Next to the chair was a dark, rectangular box. *That's what the noise was,* she thought. *I kicked that.* She bent to examine the box; it was made of a thin metal and had a hinged lid. Something was protruding from one side, preventing the lid from closing completely.

The box was filled with envelopes addressed in a small, even handwriting with a backward slant. *Letters. From Robin?* Jennie remembered that Robin had been left-handed. *Probably.* She checked her watch again. *A little after ten. Just a quick look. I'll be out of here by eleven.*

Chapter Twenty-two

Jennie sat on the floor and, holding the flashlight in one hand, opened the first envelope and removed its contents: a piece of lined notebook paper, folded into a neat rectangle. The outside was decorated with an intricate design made from the intertwined letters *R* and *B*. Struck by the grace and delicacy of the design, she studied the swirling curves briefly before she unfolded the paper and saw a variation of the design, an elaborate scroll of hearts and flowers, drawn around the edge of the paper, framing the message in the center:

> *Please don't be so hard on Daddy. He thinks I've changed because of you. And, in a way, he's right. I AM a different person since I met you. But he's wrong to think I would be the same if I didn't see you anymore. I can't EVER go back to being the same person again—I don't want to. HE wouldn't want me to if only I could make him understand how much happier I am now.*

She felt a reluctant sympathy for the young lovers and read on:

> *You won't believe what he said to me after you left. He told me he would rather see me dead than have me lose my immortal soul. Don't laugh. He really believes that's what is happening.*

She reread the last three sentences, shaking her head in disbelief, before she refolded the paper and put it back inside the envelope.

She opened another envelope and removed another letter; this one was bordered with a forest of trees whose branches and roots grew together into an embrace, cradling the same *R* and *B*.

I'm sorry about last night—sorry for the things I said and sorry you feel the way you do about Web. It's not what you think. I do love him but not in the same way I love you. Why can't you believe that? But even loving you as I do, I can't stop seeing Web. Not just because of my parents. Web is my friend and he needs help. He needs ME. If you knew his mother, you would understand.

She held the letter a few seconds, thinking about Web's mother, Leda Barrons, Riverview's director of volunteers and a tiger of a woman. Leda spoiled her only son in many ways, but expected perfection of him. Jennie put the letter aside and vowed to discover the reason for the young man's need of Robin's help.

The next letter had a border of small birds carrying a ribbon encircling the *R* and *B*.

Please be patient. Try to understand, just because I love you, I can't stop loving my father. I know you think he's a crazy old fanatic, but there's more to it than that. God is real to him. So is Hell. I DO want to marry you, but I don't want to break his heart—or my mother's. You should see how torn apart she is when Daddy and I fight. Please give me the time I need. And don't worry—no one will make me stop loving you—EVER.

And then an envelope containing a note scribbled on a torn scrap—no hearts, no flowers, no lovebirds, no interlaced initials—just the words:

You're right. After what happened with T. C. . . .

Jennie's hand shook; the circle of light convulsed into wide arcing loops. She pushed the switch with her thumb and breathed deeply, blinking back tears. T. C. Tom Connors. *Is that who she means? Has to be. So she told Brad! What did he do?* Knowing she'd find no answer in the dark, she turned the light on again and continued to read:

> . . . *I have to get away from here. But I can't leave until the end of the summer. Daddy will never forgive me. After we do this, I may never see my parents again. Let me have this summer with them. I'll go to New Orleans with you in August—as soon as school starts. I'd be leaving then anyway. I need this summer with Web too. I think he's almost ready to deal with his problem. In August, when he goes to school, he'll be away from his mother. It will be much easier for him.*

Web again. What problem? Jennie reached for the next envelope. An intricate pattern outlining the letters *R* and *B* decorated its borders, but the soft curving forms of nature had been replaced by a more angular design:

> *I wish you would stop blaming my father for everything. Try to look at this from my point of view. Daddy's no worse than Emma. He's just more honest. If anyone stops us from getting married, it will be her. You should see the way she looks at me sometimes—never when she knows you might see her—she's too smart for that. She'll try to stop me from taking you away from here. You just wait and see.*

Jennie shook her head, reluctantly drawn into empathy with Robin. She turned off the flashlight, stood up, went to the window and looked out, wondering who had been in that other car. "There's no reason to be afraid. Whoever it was is gone now." She spoke aloud, needing to hear a human voice. "The answer's here. In the letters. I'm sure of that." She looked at her watch—quarter to eleven. *Just a few more,* she told herself. *Eleven. I'll be out of here by eleven.* She returned to her position on the floor and picked up another envelope. She opened the page and saw the *R* and *B* centered at the top, now held fast in the tentacles of a vine with heart-shaped leaves, supported by grinning wood sprites dancing around the words on the page.

I have a plan now—and I know it will work. Mrs. Deighton's going to help us.

Mrs. Deighton? Jennie looked away for a moment, trying to imagine how her cousin, prim and proper Ellen, could be involved.

I'll tell my parents I'm babysitting for the little Deighton girl overnight and then we can leave for New Orleans. That will give us time. We'll be married before Daddy suspects anything. And once we're married, there's nothing he can do. I'll explain everything in a letter. Mrs. Deighton will give the letter to my mother and stay with her when she reads it. I feel so much better about that. I've really been worried about what Mother will do when she learns that I'm gone but now at least I know she'll have Mrs. Deighton with her, someone she can talk to. I'm so relieved that the details are working out.

The handwriting on the next envelope was different. The small neat letters were replaced by an uneven scrawl; the envelope was filled with torn bits of paper. Why, Jennie wondered, had this one been torn up? The others were so carefully preserved. She lay the flashlight in her lap so her hands were free to assemble the torn pieces on the floor, and leaned over the scraps, fitting the ragged edges together—

"What the hell!"

Light, merged with a roar of fury, flooded the room, so bright that it was painful, momentarily blinding Jennie. The first thing she saw, when her eyes became accustomed to the glare, was the torn letter, its pieces laid out like a puzzle on the floor. She was sitting with her back to the door so that her body hid them. She recognized the angry voice as Brad's. *Don't panic. Don't panic.* She played the words in her head, mantralike, as she scooped the scraps of paper into her hand, *don't panic,* put them in her pocket, *don't panic,* and pushed them to the bottom, *don't panic,* burying them beneath the keys.

She stood and turned to face him.

He was standing by the door with one arm extended, his fingers still on the light switch. His other hand held the guitar case.

"What's going on?" He spoke softly, his anger all the more frightening for being expressed in a whisper.

Jennie removed her hand from the pocket, trying frantically to think of an explanation.

"You were at Southern Lites tonight, weren't you?" He was leaning forward now, bent slightly at the waist.

She nodded.

"I thought I saw you. Why?"

"It's a public place," she pointed out, marveling inwardly at her own calm voice.

"Ha!" The sound was a growl, not a laugh. "What're you doing here?"

Don't panic. The mantra sustained her as she watched him, forcing herself to meet his eyes. She knew he hadn't seen the letters yet, didn't know she had been reading them. *When he finds out . . .* She looked away briefly, calculating the distance between herself and the door.

He set the guitar case down and came a step closer. Now he was not directly between her and the door.

She moved so that the rocking chair was between them and rested her hands on the top rung of the ladder back, using it as a shield.

He took another step forward.

She looked directly into his eyes, trying to read his intentions. Then that noise again, the same gonglike echo that had greeted her when she entered the house, as Brad's foot collided with the metal box and the pile of envelopes, sending white rectangles scurrying across the floor. He glanced down and saw the open box, the strewn letters. His body seemed to tighten—a fist clenching.

She moved her hands to one of the lower slats of the rocker and braced herself.

"My letters!"

Jennie steadied her hands on the chair back. *Don't panic.*

He moved toward her.

She pushed the rocker as hard as she could. The top struck him in the stomach, forcing a breath from him in a surprised grunt. He bent over double and fell forward, his arms tangling in the slats of the chair. She used all her strength to push the chair so that the movement of the chair and his own attempts to rise sent him sprawling. The grunt became an enraged howl as the back of his head hit the floor.

Jennie moved sideways, made a wide arc around him, and then sprinted through the door and across the porch. She stumbled as she ran down the rough, uneven steps, quickly regained her balance, and began to move faster when she felt the level surface of the yard beneath her feet. By the time she reached the road, she was running hard.

Was he following? She didn't know. Her shoes thudded on the road surface, drowning out all other sound. Her eyes were straight ahead, her energy focused on planting each foot solidly so she would not slip on the loose gravel. Finally she reached the car. Inside, with the doors securely locked, she allowed herself to look back. Her breath came in short choppy bursts, each one burning her lungs as she expelled it. She leaned her head on the seat back, forcing herself to take long, deep breaths, all the while keeping her eyes on the rearview mirror. The area was dimly visible by the moon's light. There was no sign of a pursuer. At least as far as the curve, the road was clear. *What if he comes through the woods?* She lifted her head to look in that direction. *He can't do that. The underbrush is too thick.*

She lay her head back again. Okay. What next? She looked at her watch: 11:25. She remembered the intruder in the car and, praying silently and vaguely—*Please God, Please God*—she extended her hand toward the floor. "Thank you, Thank you. I know I don't deserve it, but thank you!" she said aloud when her fingers touched the familiar worn leather. She reached in the purse. Her wallet was there. So far, so good. Now to get out of here. As long as I'm in the car, I'm safe. She fumbled in her pocket for the keys, selected the one she needed, and put it in the ignition. No response. Darn! She thought again of the intruder, remembered the shadowed movements and the dull thud. She tried again to start the car.

Nothing.

Chapter Twenty-three

Now what? The phone. *Who to call? The police?* She shuddered. *I'd rather walk. Kate? No. I can't ask her to drag the kids out of bed. Information. They'll have the number of an all-night towing service.* She groped in the seat beside her. *Where is it? Did I leave it in my purse?* She searched through the purse as well as she could in the dark, enough to know the phone was not there. She remembered the outline of the bulky figure leaning into the car. *Don't panic.* She checked the door locks again. *Safe. For the moment. Can't stay here all night. Think!*

She reached overhead and pushed the button that turned off the door light. *Okay. Here goes.* She kept her hand on the rearview mirror, turning it so she never lost her view of the area behind the car, and moved across the seat to the door nearest the woods. Her fingers on the door lock, she peered into the moonlit area around the car. *Now or never.* She checked the mirror again before she opened the door and slid out, keeping as low as possible. Outside, she eased the car door shut, careful to make no sound, and then crawled the few feet to the line of shadow cast by the trees.

She stood, zipped her light jacket, and put her hands in her pockets. A soft whoosh above made her look up. Whatever it was had disappeared. An owl, she told herself, hoping it was not a bat—or worse. She walked along the side of the road, avoiding the gravel, letting the grass muffle her footsteps. As she approached the curve of the road, she slowed down, unsure what lay beyond.

A swath of yellow light dissected the road and penetrated the woods opposite the house. *That means Brad's door's still open. Is he out here?* Jennie stood at the edge of the lighted strip. *I have to go through that,* she thought, looking down into the light as if it were a swift-moving river, deep and dangerous. She looked toward the cabin, but from the angle of her present position, she could see only a few feet past the open door. She did not see Brad in there. Nor could she detect any sign of him outside. Should she risk it? No choice. Shifting the heavy purse to rest more securely on her shoulder, she bent at the road's edge, picked up a handful of gravel, and threw the small stones in the direction from which she had just come. As soon as she heard them hit the hard surface of the road, she raced through the lighted area. Once on the other side, she ducked behind a tree, stood for a moment, listening, and then cautiously looked around the tree toward the small house. *There he is! On the porch!* She brought her head back behind the tree and stood rigid, debating whether to bolt or to rely on stillness and the dark of the forest to hide her. She listened for footsteps, but heard nothing. She looked again.

Brad stood on the porch, a dark shape caught between two lights, brash yellow from the house and the pale silver of the moon. Moonlight reflected off his face, his hands, and something else—some odd shape that caught the light, distorting and magnifying the shape of his hands. The letters. *He's holding the letters in his hands.* Against all logic, she stayed there, watching until he turned, went back into the house, and closed the door. She waited another few minutes, and then returned to the road and walked along its side, ready to seek cover among the trees if necessary.

Nothing turned out the way I planned, she thought. *Still, I did learn something.* She remembered Brad's hands clutching the letters, his tragic bearing as he stood on the porch. She had no doubt about the intensity of his feelings for Robin. But what did it mean? That he could never harm her? That he would never let her go?

So tired. She didn't know how far she'd walked or how far she had to go. She knew there were no houses on this road. *At the crossroad though . . . the house with the flowers . . . late to be knocking on someone's door . . . but the flowers . . . nature lovers are usually kind . . . if there's a light, I'll stop and ask for help.* But the farmhouse was dark. The flowers, eerie Munchkin faces in the moonlight, watched as she passed. No help from Oz.

On the main road, she squinted into the night, looking for the neon fireworks of Southern Lites. *Guess it's further than I remembered.* She trudged on. Then she saw the dark outline of the sign, the fireworks stripped of their color. *They're closed.* She stared at the sign. *What now?* She stood in the parking lot wondering where else she could go.

She walked around to the back and was relieved to see the lights in the living quarters were still on. She knocked on the door through which Sheila had let her out earlier.

"Hello," she said when Zac answered the door, "I'm sorry to bother you so late but I've had car trouble and—"

"Who is it?" She recognized Sheila's voice and then her round face, stripped of makeup, appeared over Zac's shoulder.

Jennie smiled at her. "I don't know if you remember, but I was here earlier this evening. You let me out the back door."

"I remember. Come on in."

Zac cut his wife off. "You say you had car trouble?"

"Yes, I—"

Sheila said, "You look like you could use something hot, honey. How about coffee?"

Jennie hesitated, distracted by the interruption and by Zac's abrupt departure from the room.

"Coffee?" Sheila repeated.

"No. Thanks anyway. I thought you might know of an all-night garage. Or a taxi? Somebody who'd be willing to drive me back to Memphis?"

Sheila looked doubtful. "Maybe Zac . . ."

Zac returned.

"Honey, you know anybody who can give this girl a ride back to Memphis?"

"Give me a minute," he said. "I'm sure there's someone. In the meantime, have some coffee. Maybe a shot of brandy. You look like you could use it."

Jennie glanced down; small particles of leaves formed a mosaic on the mud-stained knees of her jeans.

"I slipped on some loose gravel," she explained, though no one had asked.

Deaf to Jennie's protests, Sheila filled a large mug with coffee.

"How about that brandy?" Zac asked. Without waiting for a response, he poured a stream of rich brown liquid into the coffee.

Jennie breathed the warm fragrance rising from the cup, took a sip, and was glad they had not listened to her. She smiled her appreciation. All the while her mind raced, trying to think what she would do if Zac did not know anyone who would drive her home. A loud knock on the door startled her. Sheila looked surprised too.

Zac opened the door. "Smitty! To what do we owe the pleasure?" His voice was hearty, theatrical.

"Had a report of someone on foot wandering around the area," the police sergeant answered, coming into the room. "You seen or heard anything unusual?" He looked from Zac to Jennie. "Surprised to see you here, Mrs. Connors. You our unidentified wanderer?"

Despite what he said, Jennie didn't think he looked surprised. "I had car trouble," she said.

"We were just trying to think of someone who might give her a ride to Memphis," Zac said. "Any ideas?"

Sergeant Smith looked at the floor, and then at Jennie. "My shift's almost over. I'll be glad to drive you—"

"Oh, no. I'm sure it would be out of your way."

In his good-natured, amiable way, Smith brushed aside all objections.

Tom had a cup of tea waiting when Jennie came out of the shower. She dodged past him and sat on the edge of the bed, ignoring him, though the tea was tempting.

"Can we at least talk?" he said. "This . . . what you're doing . . . won't solve anything."

As much as she did not want to talk to Tom, Jennie felt an urgency to put the night's events into words. She began tentatively, speaking more to herself than him, "When this whole thing started, nothing made sense. I kept trying to piece it together. The thing I could never understand was why. There's always supposed to be a motive. But what motive could anyone have to kill a sweet little thing like Robin? That's how I'd always thought of her. And our car? How does that fit in? Then I found out about the two of you and . . . there must be a connection."

"He must have found out," Tom said. "Was jealous. And killed her. "

"That's the most obvious answer. But I can't picture him doing that. He's always seemed to me like a throwback to another era . . . a flower child. But when I really thought about it, I realized I don't know Brad. Maybe his quiet is not gentleness at all. Maybe it's anger. Smoldering. Just waiting for a spark to set it off." She leaned back against a pillow, remembering those awful moments in the cabin. "I'll never forget his face when . . ." She shuddered, reached for the cup, and holding it in both hands, breathed the lemony scent. The fragrant steam reminded her of the brandy-laced coffee and the scene in the rooms behind Southern Lites. She jerked herself upright, almost spilling the tea. "Zac called the police."

"What?"

"Remember . . . I told you how Sergeant Smith showed up out of the blue and insisted on giving me a ride home. Well, just before that, Zac left the room for a few minutes. And when Smitty . . . that's what they all call him . . . came to the door . . . Zac's greeting seemed phony. He must have called the police while she was making the coffee." She took a sip of tea. "I wonder why."

"Smith didn't say?"

"He said somebody reported a stranger in the area."

"Maybe they did."

"If they did, it wasn't me. I'm sure nobody saw me. I kept in the shadows. Anyway, no cars passed."

"I still don't understand why you went up there."

"I wondered if he really loved Robin. She could have been one of many for him. Just another groupie. At least that's what I thought before tonight." She set the cup on the table beside the bed. "So I decided to go and watch him while he was working. Observe him in his natural habitat, so to speak."

"That makes sense. Going into his house . . . that doesn't."

She didn't bother to look at him. "I don't owe you an explanation." But, because she needed words to clarify her actions for herself, she explained anyway. "Once I got to Southern Lites, I realized most of the people in the place were regulars. I knew there was no way I could avoid Brad's noticing me. And if he knew he was being observed, he'd be on his guard."

"Against what?"

She ignored the question. "So when Sheila let me out the back door, I jumped at the chance. As to going to his house . . ." An elaborate shrug, and then: "An impulse. I was so close, I thought I'd go to his place and look around. I didn't intend to go inside. That just . . . well, one thing led to another."

"Did you find anything?"

She had already decided not to tell him about the letters. "I saw a side of Brad I'd never seen before."

"You're lucky you got out of there alive."

"He didn't follow me. Once I was outside he didn't even try to catch me."

"Maybe he called the police."

She thought about this, and shook her head. "No, I'm sure it was Zac. But why?"

"Who knows? But you're probably right that it was Zac. Brad seems like the type to go it alone. Not ask for help from anyone, especially the police."

"Let's hope so. I don't want to explain to Goodley what I was doing in his house. I wish I knew how much Smith knows. What he's told Goodley."

"From now on, stay away from River County. Leave the detecting to Goodley."

Jennie had too much else on her mind to challenge his commanding tone. "He's probably found the car by now. I'll have to explain that."

"Promise me you'll stay out of this."

When Jennie did not answer, Tom leaned down and put his hand under her chin, forcing her to look at him. "Jennie, promise."

She jerked away.

He was shaking now. "Jennie, I want you to stop this."

Her anger matched his. "Don't tell me what to do."

"I'm not telling you what to do. I'm asking."

"Well, don't. You've forfeited that right."

He went to the window and stood with his back to her, staring out into the darkness. After a moment in which the only sound was the steady hum of the air conditioner, he turned. "You lied to me about the movie, Jen. That's not like you."

Only the knowledge that the kids were in the next room kept Jennie from throwing her cup at him. She glared at him, daring him to say more.

He looked away first, not accepting the dare. After a few seconds, he asked, "What's going to happen to us?"

"Us? I'm not sure there is an us anymore."

"Don't say that."

His voice was barely audible and there were tears in his eyes.

Seeing them, a wave of emotion swept over her. Robert Frost's lines about love and hate, fire and ice, came to mind. Was it love she felt? Or hate? Which was stronger? Or was pride stronger than both? She blinked back her own tears and said, "One thing at a time. How do we handle the car? Should I call a tow truck? Or the rental company? Let them take care of it."

"You didn't look under the hood?"

"For what? I don't know anything about cars. I just wanted to get out of there."

"Forget the tow truck. We'll go out there together tomorrow. Maybe I can figure out what's wrong and you can drive it back."

"A minute ago you wanted me to stay away from River County."

"This is different. I'll be with you."

Like it or not, she knew that was the best option. "Okay, tomorrow. As soon as the kids get on the bus."

Tom shook his head. "I have a presentation first thing."

"Can't someone else handle it?"

He shook his head. "The big guns are coming in from New York about that new software package. It's my baby and I have to be there."

"Well, when?"

"Afternoon, I guess. How about right after lunch?"

"I'm scheduled at Riverview."

"Can't someone cover for you?"

She gave him a long look.

"They must have a list of subs. What if one of the kids was sick?"

"You're indispensable at SAIS?"

He defended himself: "It's my head on a platter if this thing doesn't fly."

She didn't press the matter. Right now, it wasn't the most important issue they had to settle. "Okay. When can you be home?"

"The presentation's first thing. I'll be here before lunch."

"It'd be a lot easier to call a tow truck."

"I'd like to check it myself. See if the car was tampered with, or was it just ordinary car trouble."

"If it was ordinary car trouble, the timing couldn't have been worse."

"I'd like to know for sure."

Jennie did not argue with that. Too tired to carry her pillow in to the couch, she turned off her lamp and stretched out, as close to her edge of the bed as she could get.

Chapter Twenty-four

Guess there's more to the lady than meets the eye," Goodley said, looking up from the papers on his desk. "Good report, by the way. Very thorough."

Smith acknowledged the compliment with a grin and finished his coffee before he spoke. "I had her pegged for a bit of fluff, myself."

"Me too," Goodley said. "Guess we were wrong. Think she was at the crime scene?"

"Nothing else back there to interest her."

"It's a long walk from that field to Southern Lights."

"I'd say she had a long walk. She was nervous as a cat when she got in the car with me, but she kept nodding off. She was that tired."

"Wonder why she wouldn't call her husband."

"I asked her that. She said something about he couldn't leave the kids alone, and she didn't want him to drag them out of bed in the middle of the night."

"You believe her?"

"Makes sense, I guess, but I had the feeling there was something else. Because she sure didn't want me to drive her home. I had to do some fast talking."

Goodley chuckled. He stood up and headed for the door. "She said she had car trouble. The car must be somewhere between the the crime scene and Southern Lites."

"Mind if I come along?"

"Sure you want to? You've been up all night. Night shift again tonight."

"I'll take my own car. If it gets too long, I'll go on home. But, yeah, I wanna come."

Goodley began to doubt his theory as they got closer to the murder scene and there was no sign of the car Jennie had been driving. Restless, he looked toward the van in the driveway when they passed Brad's place, and then back at the road, slowing down as he approached the curve just beyond the cabin. "Jackpot!" he said when he spotted the abandoned vehicle, though he wasn't a man who normally talked to himself. He gave a jubilant thumbs-up signal to Smith, following in the car behind him, and pulled over to the side of the road.

Smith pulled in behind him. "You were right," he said.

Goodley was already walking around the car, eyes squinted as he looked through the windows and checked the doors. "Well, at least she's learned to lock her doors," he said, as he tested the doors on the left-hand side.

Smith was in front of the car. When Goodley joined him, he gestured toward the hood, which was not tightly closed. Goodley acknowledged this with a nod and raised eyebrows, but said nothing. He continued his walk around the car, stopping beside the right front door.

"Look at this." Like the hood, this door was closed, but not latched. "She locked both doors on the other side." He paused and looked at the right rear door. "Back door, this side. But not the front. Didn't even close it all the way."

"So, what're you thinking?" Smith asked.

"She exited the car from this side. My guess is she was in a hurry."

"What about the hood?"

"That figures. Most people have car trouble, they check under the hood. She couldn't tell what the problem was, so she closed it, but didn't slam it."

Smith was doubtful. "I don't see her as anyone who would even look under the hood."

"What was she doing here in the first place? That's the real question."

"Any theories?" Smith asked.

"Not yet." Hands deep in his pockets, Goodley continued to look at the car. "I'm going to check the crime scene. You coming?"

"Wouldn't miss it for the world."

Goodley looked at the three cars again, and said to Smith. "We'll walk the rest of the way. You move your car around to the front of hers, pull in tight, I'll move mine closer in back."

"Block her in?"

Goodley nodded. "I don't want that car moved before we get back."

After both men had moved their cars, they followed the narrow road to the spot where Robin's body had been discovered.

"Any idea what we're looking for?" Smith asked, as they ducked under the sagging yellow ribbons.

"If she was here, I figure there'll be signs."

Starting at the outer perimeter of the cordoned area, the two of them continued in narrowing circles, heads down, without speaking. Smith broke the silence. "Well, there are plenty of signs of someone or something. But it could have been anything, four-legged or two."

Goodley grunted.

The circles became smaller.

There was a yelp of triumph from Goodley. "Look at this," he said, holding aloft a small object for Smith to see. He turned the bangle around in his fingers, examining it from every angle, and then slipped it into a pocket as he and Smith went back to where they'd left their cars.

After sending Smith home, Goodley settled in for the wait, passing the time by going over the notes on his clipboard. From time to time he picked up the small object and looked at it thoughtfully.

Chapter Twenty-five

Jennie retrieved the *Commercial Appeal* from the prickly branches of the pyracantha and waited for Kate to answer the doorbell. "Trade you this for a cup of tea," she offered, holding the newspaper aloft when Kate appeared, still in her robe.

"Good grief, what are you doing out at this hour?"

"I drove the kids to school."

"I thought the guidance counselor told you not to hover."

"They're not her kids." Jennie handed over the paper and followed Kate into the house.

"I can't argue with that. Enough about the kids. Tell me about last night. Why didn't you call?"

"Your lights were out, so I figured—"

Kate waved the explanation short, "Just tell me what happened."

She filled her cheeks with air, blew it out. "I'll need a cup of tea."

Kate laughed. "This better be good, Jen."

"Good isn't exactly the word I'd use."

"What happened?"

She held up one finger. "In a minute. First I have to call Riverview. Let them know I won't be in today."

The tea became lukewarm, and then ice cold, while she filled Kate in on the details, including the secret it hurt most to share: Tom's relationship with Robin, ending with, "Now can you see why I have to find out for myself what happened?"

"Not necessarily. I still think you should back off and let Goodley do his job." There was a long pause before Kate added, "You don't think there's any possibility—"

"No." Jennie's reply was swift and adamant.

"Have you asked him?"

"Of course I did. The morning he told me about it." She paused, biting her lip. *It.* That little word we use to describe anything too horrendous to name. "In spite of everything, I believe him. About the murder anyway."

"Who do you think—"

"I wish I knew. Maybe Brad."

"How can you be so sure about Tom?"

Jennie shrugged. "I'm going on instinct there."

"But your instincts didn't tell you . . ." Kate's voice drifted.

"I know. Still, I think Brad has the most reason." She refused to admit, even to Kate, how shaky her belief in her own instinct had become.

Kate said, "I don't know. From what you've told me about those letters, it could be several other people. Even, God forbid, her own father."

"Who else would have a reason to set up Tom? Or me?"

Kate gave her a sharp look. "I wondered if you'd thought of that."

"How could I not?"

"I still say leave it to Goodley."

"I've got a lot more incentive than he has."

"You're also a lot more vulnerable." Kate leaned across the table. "Face it, Jen! You're going after a killer."

"I know." Jennie toyed with her spoon, deliberately avoiding Kate's eyes. "I'm thinking about getting a gun."

"Get serious."

Jennie hunched her shoulders. "I know how to shoot. Dad taught me when I was a kid." She stopped and made a mock gun with her finger and thumb. "I got pretty good at knocking cans off a fence post."

Kate hooted at that. "I don't believe this. You, of all people. Miss Gun Control Fanatic. You're too close to this. Losing perspective."

Jennie shrugged. "It's just an idea." She glanced up at the clock. "I better get going. I have a ton of things to do before Tom gets home. And then we have to drive out there to get the car." She grimaced. "I'm not looking forward to that."

"I don't blame you. Call me if you need anything."

"Don't I always? Thanks for the tea and"—she moved an expressive hand through the air—"for being there for me. There's no way to repay somebody for that."

Kate grinned mischievously. "Maybe your diamond earrings?"

"Now who's losing perspective?"

When she got home, Jennie went to the family Bible and took out the one letter she had not told even Kate about. She smoothed the page flat, running her thumb over the tape holding the pieces together, and read:

I know it's hard for you to understand but please try. We have to wait. Everything's so complicated right now. I saw Tom Connors yesterday at the drugstore and I think he hates me. First he pretended he didn't see me and then, when I went toward him, he almost ran out the door. I think he's afraid I'll tell his wife what happened. But I know how he feels about his family and I want him to know that what happened will never be a threat to them. And I want to tell him about us—you and me. I want him to know I've found someone of my own and I'm happy now, but every time I see him, he runs away. I can't start a new life until this is settled.

Jennie read the note several times; each time the words seemed to mean something different. It could have been the spark that set Brad off. Read differently, it looked bad for Tom. She tried to imagine how it would sound to Goodley. *Let's hope he never sees it.* She thought of her statement to Kate and wished she really felt that sure of Tom's innocence. She put the reconstructed letter back in the Bible and spent the rest of the morning catching up on things starting to slide now that she had a job. It took every ounce of discipline she had to leave the letter between the pages and complete her tasks.

"There. That's where he lives," Jennie said later that day when she and Tom passed Brad's house. The only evidence of his presence was a pair of jeans on a clothesline. "I hope we don't run into him."

"Yeah," Tom agreed. "Are we getting close to the car?"

"Mm-hmm. It's just past—" They rounded the curve after Brad's home. "Jeez!"

There was the gray Jetta, with Goodley sitting behind the wheel. Tom glanced at her. "What're you going to tell him?"

"The truth. What else? There's no law against my being here."

"What about breaking and entering?"

"I'm hoping that doesn't come up." *And praying. And crossing everything crossable.*

He gave her a quick, incredulous look, and then swung wide around both the Jetta and the vehicle in front of it. Once past, he made a U-turn, bringing his car nose to nose with the rental car.

"What're you doing?" Jennie asked.

"Maybe it's just a dead battery and we can jump-start it."

"Can't be that simple."

"Doesn't hurt to try."

"Look at him." Jennie nodded toward Goodley, fuming. "He's waiting for us to come to him. That arrogant . . ." She stopped. None of the words in her normal vocabulary were adequate.

"He's just doing his job," Tom, ever reasonable, pointed out.

"Don't say that to me! Somebody's always telling me he's just doing his job. If he were really doing his job, this murder would be solved. But there he sits. Like the Great Poobah! Well, I'm not going to him. If he wants to talk to me, he's going to have to come here." She settled back into the seat, trying to look composed. When she saw Goodley's door open, she brushed some loose hair back from her face with nervous fingers.

"Hello," she said, when he leaned down to look at her.

Goodley wasted no time. "Tell me about last night."

She said, "What do you want to know?"

"For starters, why did you visit the crime scene in the middle of the night?"

That stopped her. "I didn't."

"I have reason to believe you did."

"No. Let me explain what happened." Inwardly she tried to shore up her crumbling resolve.

"The truth will save us both a lot of time."

"Well," she began, hoping that he had not talked to Brad, "I went to Southern Lites last night. Then, when I left . . . I left by the back door because this guy . . ."

Goodley nodded when she said this.

"Somehow I got confused. Maybe because I left by a different door. I took a wrong turn. Then I had car trouble. I ended up leaving the car. Here. It is close to the crime scene, but . . . Have you talked to Sergeant Smith? He gave me a ride home."

"I have his full report."

"He must have told you I had car trouble."

"He said that's what you told him."

There was no inflection of any kind in Goodley's voice, at least none Jennie could read. She said, "Well, that's what happened."

"After Smitty told me about you showing up at Southern Lites in the middle of the night, I had a hunch you'd been here and decided to take a little ride. I saw the car." He paused and pointed to the area just in front of them, where Tom was looking under the hood of the rental car. "I recognized it as the one you've been driving, and then I proceeded back to the spot where the body was discovered."

He paused, as though waiting for her to speak.

She said nothing.

"I found this"—he held out his hand, revealing a gold bracelet—"in one of the tire tracks left by your car." He turned the bangle so that the letters *J E N* were clearly visible.

Her stomach was doing flips, but somehow she managed to keep her voice level. "That's mine," she said, "but I haven't been back there since that day. I must have lost it then."

"What day?"

"A couple of days after I found the body, when I went back to look around. You saw me," she reminded him.

Goodley was shaking his head.

"You don't remember that?"

"I remember just fine, but this"—he held the bracelet at her eye level—"wasn't there then, nor even as recently as two days ago."

Tom came over to them, saw the bracelet in Goodley's hand, and asked, "What's going on?"

Goodley turned to him. "Where were you last night?"

"Home. With our kids."

"Anybody else?"

"No."

"What time do your kids go to bed?"

Jennie had to interrupt. "He'd never leave them alone."

Goodley studied both of them, and finally said, "I want to know exactly what happened last night."

Jennie took her time relaying a carefully edited version of the previous night to the policeman. At the same time, she was going over the past couple of weeks in her mind, trying to remember the last time she'd worn the bracelet. She mentioned her unauthorized visit to Brad's cabin, figuring he'd find out about it anyway. The letters, however, she kept to herself.

"That's it?" Goodley asked when she finished.

She nodded.

"You're sure you weren't wearing the bracelet last night?"

"Positive."

"You couldn't be mistaken?"

She shook her head.

"Any idea the last time you saw it?"

"No." Her mind was whirling. *Somebody put it there. Somebody who has access to my things. Who? Why?* There was no time to think about that now. Goodley was demanding her full attention.

"There's nothing else you want to tell me?"

"I can't think of anything."

"In other words, you didn't find anything in that cabin that would make it worth my while to obtain a search warrant?"

Jennie, caught off guard by his question, didn't answer immediately.

"Off the record," he added.

His manner was too ingratiating, setting off alarm bells in her head. *He knows there's more. Just keep it simple.* Aloud, she said, "No."

He turned to Tom. "How about you? Is there anything you'd like to add?"

Tom looked the other man straight in the eye and shook his head. He did not look at Jennie.

She wondered if Goodley noticed the strain between her and Tom. By now, she knew him well enough to know he didn't miss much. She braced herself for more questions, and was relieved when he asked Tom, "What about the car?"

"Spark plug wires."

"Disconnected?"

Tom nodded.

Goodley turned to Jennie. "You didn't try to reconnect them?"

"How was I supposed to know?"

"You didn't look under the hood?"

"No."

"Didn't you even try to determine what was wrong?"

"I wouldn't know where to start."

Tom went back to the car during this exchange, and after a few minutes, slammed the hood down.

Jennie jumped. "That's what I heard," she said. Goodley didn't look like he understood, so she elaborated. "Last night, when I was standing on the porch."

"And you can't describe the person you saw?"

"No. I told you. It was too dark."

"And you didn't recognize the vehicle?"

"No. But I know it wasn't Brad's van. Or a pickup truck."

"A pickup truck?" Goodley asked, suddenly alert as a cat on snow.

"Like the one following me," she reminded him.

Chapter Twenty-six

Idon't see why we can't ride the bus like everybody else."

Jennie half-listened to the grumbling of her eldest son as she checked the rearview mirror, and then surveyed the parking lot before opening the car door.

"Mom! You're not going in with us!"

"Relax, Tommy. If you don't make a big deal out of it, nobody else will."

Despite Tommy's protests, she stayed with her sons all the way to their respective classrooms.

On her way back to the car, she scanned the area again, checking for a green pickup. *Nowhere in sight. That's good.* She slid behind the wheel, started the engine, and looked around one last time. At the far end of the lot, partially hidden by the dumpster, was a white station wagon. The driver slouched behind the wheel and ducked his bald head when Jennie looked toward him. *He's hiding!* She rested her chin on the steering wheel, thinking. *Should I? Do I have a choice?* She shook her head. *I have to make him listen.*

She made the drive to Riverview in record time. *Good, he's here.* She pulled into the empty slot beside Goodley's car. Inside, she walked quickly past the main desk, through the doors leading to the East Wing.

She stopped at the nurses' station and asked, "Lieutenant Goodley in there?" She nodded toward E46, Edward Pynchon's room. "I need to talk to him."

"Yes, he's here, hanging around waiting for Mr. Pynchon to say something."

"He still hasn't spoken?"

"Not a word."

"Do the doctors expect him to come around?"

The nurse shrugged. "Nobody seems to know quite what the problem is. He's conscious now, alert, just doesn't talk."

"Has he had any visitors? Except Goodley?"

"Yep. Two. Same two. Every day.

"Do you know who they are?"

"That woman who found him after the accident and some guy, fairly young, red hair, ponytail, beard."

Jennie remembered Brad and Emma leaving Pynchon's room the day Goodley had taken her to see him. "Are they here now?" she asked.

"Not yet. But they usually come by in the morning, so they'll probably be here soon."

She thought a minute, and then said, "How about a favor?"

"What do you have in mind?"

"I really need to talk to Goodley, preferably not in that room. I don't want to upset Mr. Pynchon again. Isn't there something you could do to get Goodley out of there for a few minutes?"

"Sure. Mr. Pynchon hasn't had his bath yet. I'll ask the aide to do him next. The cop always goes for coffee while we bathe him."

"Perfect."

The nurse left her station to speak to a stocky man dressed in green scrubs. He looked at Jennie, flashed her a grin, and headed toward Room E46.

"Thanks," Jennie said when the nurse came back. "I'll owe you big time for this one."

"I'm gonna hold you to that."

She watched Goodley enter the hall and head for the coffee machine. When she approached, he was feeding a dollar bill into a slot. "Got a minute?" she asked.

He looked a little surprised to see her. "I thought Friday was your day off."

"You're right. I'm not on the job now. I'm here because I need to talk to you."

"Oh?"

She took a deep breath and jumped right in. "Someone's stalking my kids."

He didn't respond.

"The green pickup truck, the one I told you about yesterday, I've seen it several times. And today there was a white station wagon hiding behind the dumpster in the school parking lot. That guy was sitting in it."

"What guy?"

"The guy who was driving the pickup truck."

"What makes you think it's the same one?" Goodley kept his eyes on his coffee, a departure from his usual intimidating look-you-in-the-eye gaze.

"It is. I know. But this morning he was in a different car, a station wagon, white. And he was hiding."

"How do you know that?"

"There's no other explanation. And that picture I told you about . . ." She paused, removed an envelope from her purse, and gave it to Goodley.

He glanced inside the envelope, and then at Jennie.

"You didn't even look!"

He removed the curling piece of paper from the envelope and held it up between two fingers. "There's not much to see."

"I found it in Tommy's pocket; he told me a man at the bus stop had taken his and Andy's picture."

"I don't know what you want me to do."

"Every time I pass the school, I see the same green truck, and the same man. Only this morning he was in a different car. But I'm sure it's the same guy. At school he pretends he's working with the land-scapers."

"Pretends?"

She ignored the sarcasm. "And I've seen him, I know it's him, hanging around the sewer construction near my kids' bus stop."

"Maybe he works two jobs."

"But he's never working. He's always . . . just there."

"No laws have been broken."

Jennie had the feeling she was being brushed off and tried another tack. "Isn't it a policy to check on anyone loitering around a school?"

"He's not loitering. He's working." Goodley's tone was mild, dismissive.

"I am not imagining this." She leaned closer as she spoke, daring him to ignore her.

"A pickup truck? Green?"

She nodded.

"And now a white station wagon?"

"Yes."

"When you told me about the stranger you watched from Brad Wilson's porch, you specifically said the vehicle was not a truck."

"Okay," she admitted. "That was a different vehicle."

"Was it the station wagon?"

"No."

"What was it?"

"A sedan. Fairly late model. That's the best I can do."

"And yet you're so sure about the truck? And now this other vehicle, the white station wagon. But the car that night, no idea at all?"

"I only saw an outline."

"Didn't see the color?"

She shook her head. "How could I in the dark?" *You're going to have to deal with this, Buddy. Because I'm not giving up.*

He studied her through narrowed eyes. "Tell you what," he said. "You write down everything suspicious, including a description of any questionable persons or vehicles. Don't leave out anything. Give me a complete report."

"Don't patronize me."

"I—"

"You'll take my report, file it neatly away, and forget about it. If you don't just toss it immediately."

Goodley's expression was impossible to read, but at least now she had his attention.

"My kids are in danger!"

"I'm sure you believe that."

"I wouldn't be here if I didn't."

He looked away first. "I have to get back now," he said. "You bring me that report as soon as you finish."

She found a quiet corner in the dining hall and started digging for a pen. *Everything in here but what I really need.* She gave the large shoulder bag one last shake and headed out into the hall.

Having worked as a volunteer before joining the staff, she knew there would be yellow pads in the Volunteer Services office. When she reached the closed door, muffled voices, obviously in conflict, made her reluctant to go in. She recognized one as belonging to Leda Barrons, Director of Volunteer Services. The other, she was pretty sure, belonged to Leda's son, Web. Phrases from one of Robin's letters came back to her: *Web's problem* and *If you knew his mother, you'd understand.*

She stepped away from the door when she heard footsteps coming down the hall. "Hi," she said, when she saw it was someone from the billing office, and hoped it wasn't apparent she'd been eavesdropping. "I need a pen and some paper. Can you help me?"

"Sure."

She returned to the quiet spot in the dining hall and began filling the lined pages of the steno pad with her small, neat handwriting. *Be specific. Not too dramatic. Don't want him to think I'm hysterical.*

"Sugar. No cream. Right?"

She looked up and was surprised to see Goodley standing at the other side of the table, holding out a styrofoam cup.

"Thought you might like some coffee," he said. "I always have a cup when I do my reports."

She accepted the offering, wondering what he was up to.

"How's it going?" He gestured toward the steno pad and sat opposite her. He sounded concerned, almost solicitous.

Warning bells were shrilling in her head, but she continued to write, phrasing each thought carefully. When she finished, she pushed the pad across the table. "I think I've covered everything. If you have any questions, you know how to reach me."

"Stick around a minute. I'll look it over now."

He held the notebook in front of him, but Jennie was sure he wasn't reading her words. He kept glancing toward the door. After an awkward five minutes he stood. She turned around to see Brad and Emma entering the room.

Emma stopped abruptly when she saw Jennie. "What's she doing here? That why you asked us to come down and have a cup of coffee?"

Goodley motioned them to join him and Jennie at the table. When everyone was seated, he said to Brad, "I understand Mrs. Connors paid you a little visit the other night."

Brad gave Jennie a sidelong glance but said nothing.

Jennie tried frantically to remember exactly what she had told Goodley about that night in the cabin.

Goodley looked at each of them in turn, letting the silence build. Finally he asked Brad, "Why didn't you report the incident to me?"

"Report it?"

"That's what people usually do when their home is broken into." Goodley spoke rapidly but precisely, enunciating each syllable of each word.

"I didn't think it was necessary."

"When the law is broken, you have a duty to report it to the police." Goodley looked from Brad to Jennie and back again.

"Nothing was stolen."

"Your home was illegally—"

Emma stood up, literally bouncing on her toes. "Will someone please tell me what this is all about?"

Ignoring her, Goodley continued to focus on Brad. "Are you aware that you have a right to press charges against this woman?" He looked pointedly toward Jennie.

"I don't want —"

Emma appeared ready to explode. "Do you mean to say that this little snip"—she paused to turn a baleful eye on Jennie—"broke into the cabin while he was—"

"Please, Emma," Brad interrupted.

"You're too easy," Emma said. She stood abruptly and turned to Goodley. "How about me? Can I press charges?"

Goodley looked surprised.

"Well, can I?" Emma persisted. "I'm the owner of the cabin so, technically, she broke into my property."

"Do you want to press charges?" Goodley asked.

Jennie thought he seemed uncomfortable.

"No, she doesn't," Brad said. He lay his hand on Emma's arm and shook his head. "You'd just make it worse."

"Well, somebody should do something." Emma sat down again. "Everything that's happened is because of her."

That really caught Goodley's attention. "How's that?"

"I don't know," Emma said, rising from her chair again. "Robin Langley's dead, not that I ever thought much of her, but—"

"Emma!" Brad was white-faced.

"Well, it's the truth. You knew I didn't like the girl but, still, it's a shame she ended up like she did. And . . ." Emma turned to Jennie and continued, her eyes glowing like those of an Old Testament prophet, "And poor Edward, look what happened to him, all because he wanted to protect you."

Protect me? That was a new thought.

The echo of an overturned metal wastebasket distracted them.

"Sorry 'bout that."

Brad's hands clinched into fists when he saw Web Barrons.

Web set the wastebasket right and then turned to his mother, who was three steps behind him. "You don't have to follow me. I can get my own coffee."

"Three-ring circus," Emma said.

When she spoke, Web appeared to notice the group at the table for the first time. He gave his mother a wicked grin and ambled over to join them. "How's the investigation going?"

Goodley ignored the question. "I see you've recovered from the accident."

"How'd you hear about it?"

Goodley didn't respond to that either. "Your car?"

"Totaled."

Protect me? Jennie couldn't get Emma's words out of her head. Web's driving misadventures didn't seem relevant at the moment. She wondered why Goodley had brought the matter up.

"What're you driving now?" Goodley asked Web.

"One of my old man's cars, most of the time a—"

Leda Barrons moved across the room with surprising speed and planted her diminutive figure between her son and Goodley. "I distinctly remember telling you to direct inquiries to any member of this family through our attorney."

"Just making conversation," Goodley said.

Right. And a spider spins a web because it's pretty.

"Nevertheless, Mr. Barrons and I would prefer—"

"Mother, I asked you not to interfere." Web was slurring his words badly.

Mrs. Barrons wheeled to face her son. "Your father and I—"

"Leave me alone, Mother! There isn't any reason not to talk to him." He turned to Goodley. "Just for the record, it was not a DUI. I wasn't even tested for alcohol."

Brad moved angrily in his chair and looked meaningfully at Emma.

"None of that concerns me. I just asked what kind of car you're driving now," Goodley reminded him.

"I drive my father's Lexus most of the time." He looked puzzled.

Jennie was beginning to understand the reason for Goodley's supposedly casual questions. If the senior Mr. Barrons drove a Lexus, it would probably be a sedan, and definitely a late model. Did that mean Goodley suspected Web of following her?

Web asked, "What does my car have to do with anything?"

"Yes, Lieutenant, I'd be interested in the answer to that," Leda asked sharply.

"Just curious," Goodley said.

Emma, hopping mad, rescued the conversation from this little side trip. "We came to visit our friend, and you, all sweetness and light, lure us down here, supposedly for coffee. I want to know the real reason."

"There have been some"—Goodley was obviously choosing his words carefully—"unusual events. And I thought a face-to-face meeting might help straighten matters out."

"What sort of events?"

"Mrs. Connors believes someone is following her and—"

"In other words, she's the reason we were all dragged down here?" Emma spat out the words.

"Are any of you following Mrs. Connors?"

Nobody bothered to answer.

What's he doing? Jennie wondered.

"What does this have to do with Robin?" Web asked. "Are you any closer to knowing who killed her?"

Goodley looked intently at each of them before he answered. "Someone seems to be deliberately interfering with the orderly course of my investigation, and"—again he looked at each of them—"I intend to find out who. And why."

"Is my son free to leave?" Leda asked.

"Everyone is free to leave," Goodley said.

"You can go too," he said to Jennie when she remained at the table after the others had gone.

"You tried to get him to press charges against me."

"My job is to uphold the law. Breaking and entering are against the law."

"I don't understand you. Yesterday, out at the car, butter wouldn't melt in your mouth." She lowered her voice, mimicking his deep baritone. "'Do you have anything you want to tell me? Off the record,' you said. What are you trying to do anyway?"

Chapter Twenty-seven

Poor Edward. All because he wanted to protect you." What did Emma mean by that? Jennie remembered the older woman's ire, the set of her shoulders, the natural grace with which she moved even when angry. Another memory clicked into place. That's it! I knew that day at Barney's I'd seen her before. She checked her watch. Time for a quick trip to Oz.

When she slowed to turn into the drive, Emma appeared, one hand on a hip, the other clutching a hooklike garden tool.

"Thought I might be seeing you," Emma said.

Jennie pasted on her best smile. "I hope it's not a bad time. I'd like—"

Emma didn't give her a chance to finish. "Charm won't work on me, young lady." There was an unmistakable dare in the thundercloud gray eyes.

Jennie realized she should have taken time to work out a plan before she came. Well, she was here now. Nothing to do but go ahead. She took a deep breath. "I want—"

"I know what you want. You want to know what I meant when I said Edward was trying to protect you."

Jennie hesitated, trying to figure out how to deal with this unpredictable person.

"If you want to know something from me, just ask. And I'll tell you. Or I won't. Depending on the question."

"Fair enough. What did you mean when you said Edward was trying to protect me?"

"I meant what I said."

"When I talked to you that day at Barney's, you never said whether or not you believed Mr. Pynchon's running into the tree was really an accident."

"Accident or not, doesn't matter."

"But if it was an accident, how could I be to blame? So, apparently, you think it wasn't."

Emma didn't answer. Instead she knelt in the black earth in front of a plot of zinnias and commenced digging.

"I'm not going to leave you alone until you answer me."

No response.

"Do you know the cause of Mr. Pynchon's accident?"

"Don't pretend you don't." Emma brandished the gardening tool like a weapon.

"I hardly knew him, so I don't know why he'd try to protect me. Or why he thought he needed to. We only met one time."

"I know that."

Jennie abandoned her attempt at polite inquiry and matched her tone to Emma's. "I think you know a whole lot more, and it's not fair—"

"Nobody's ever accused me of being unfair."

"If you know something about this murder and about your friend's accident, you—"

"I don't know anything about a murder and, technically, I don't know anything about what happened to Edward, but I've put two and two together and I know you're the cause of it."

"But why? You must have a reason."

"Like I said, two and two."

Jennie refused to give up. "That's not an answer."

Emma glared at her, chin thrust forward.

Heartened by the fact that Emma reminded her of her grandmother, Jennie grinned. "Maybe we could start over." She held out her hand.

After a long hesitation, Emma reached for it. "You're not a quitter. I'll say that for you."

Jennie detected the hint of a smile behind the gruff words.

They sat on the front steps while they talked.

Emma began slowly, "For some reason, Edward was fascinated

by that murder. Cut all the articles out of the paper, told everybody how he'd met you."

"People do that when anything sensational happens close to home."

"Not Edward. Wasn't like him," Emma argued. "This murder . . . the way he talked about it . . . always hinting he'd seen something."

"Did you ask him what?"

"Couldn't pin him down."

"Any idea why he wanted me to meet him?"

Emma hunched her shoulders and said, "The day of the funeral, he stopped by here. We watched the news together. When they showed you in front of the church, he got real excited, said now he understood."

"Understood what?"

"He didn't say."

"Didn't you ask him?"

"By that time I was sick of hearing about the whole nasty business."

In her head, Jennie ran through the sequence of events. "He didn't call me until almost two weeks after the funeral. What made him finally decide to call? Did anything else happen?"

Again, that quick drawing up of the shoulders by Emma, then quiet. After a few minutes, she said, "Don't know if anything happened, but there's no doubt in my mind there's a connection between that news report and those hints."

Jennie tried to piece together the details of the funeral. She thought about the photographer and the reporter, that dreadful woman with the glittering eyes, how they'd stopped her and Tom on their way into the church, but she'd been too wrapped up in her own feelings to wonder where else they'd turned their camera. She said to Emma, "I didn't see that news broadcast. What exactly did they show?"

"I don't remember all the details. I'd gone into the kitchen . . . Edward called me when they showed Brad standing in the street. Then, after Brad left, they showed you and some man, your husband I guess. There were other people around you. That's when he said 'now I understand.'" Emma stared into space, as though concentrating on the dust motes floating above her garden.

"Did he say anything else?"

"'I hope she'll be all right.'"

"Excuse me?"

"That's what he said. 'I hope she'll be all right.' He said it then and, after that, seems like every time they mentioned the murder on the news or he read about the investigation in the paper, he'd say that, or something like that."

"You think he meant me?"

Emma shrugged. "Who else?"

As she drove away from Emma's garden, Jennie tried to picture Edward Pynchon as she had first seen him, but she could only remember an outline, the details of the man obscured by the shade of a twisted willow tree. She remembered the high stool on which he had been perched, but not the man himself. And yet, he had remembered her. Why? More important, what might he have seen from his vantage point on that stool?

She made a gravel-churning U-turn.

Chapter Twenty-eight

At the flea market Jennie looked at the empty tables, tipped over on their sides, the tops spattered with dirt. *This is where the lamps were. The old clock was here. Mr. Pynchon's table was under a tree near the far edge of the field. About here. Yes. The stool was lying on the ground.*

After trying several times, she found that by placing the spindly legs just so, they fit into the intricate pattern of the tree roots and provided a stable foundation. Though the stool was tall enough that her feet didn't touch the ground, it was surprisingly comfortable. She leaned back, using the tree trunk for a backrest and looked over the grounds of the flea market: on one side she saw lines of overturned tables; beyond the tables, the food pavilion, smoke rising from its broad chimney

In front of the pavilion and the tables was the gravel parking lot. Her rental car was parked alone at one end. At the other end, in front of the barbecue stand, were about a dozen vehicles, mostly trucks. She surveyed this area through narrowed eyes. The stool on which she sat provided a clear view of the parking lot—now.

But what could have been seen when the tables were heaped with merchandise and the network of paths filled with people? *How tall is Edward Pynchon? Probably a little taller than I am.* She sat straighter. Yes, he would see the parking lot, especially the front row where her car had been. But, even if he saw someone get into that particular car and drive away, there would be no reason for him to pay special attention or to remember. The answer must be somewhere else.

She turned to the line of trees that formed the boundary of the market area. She knew the river was on the other side. A level path

163

lay between the gridded area of the flea market and trees. The path was actually a small road, used, she assumed, by vendors to bring trailers hauling heavy items closer to their designated spot. Peering the short distance down the road toward the parking lot, she saw nothing of interest, just a few scraps of paper caught in the weeds.

In the other direction, trees grew on both sides of the road. Squinting, she could discern a glimmer of light through the dark tunnel. She used her hand as a sun shield and saw the outline of a small building. A glint of light. A window pane? Without stopping to consider what she might find, she jogged down the overgrown road toward the building.

Darn! She looked at the large padlock, thinking wistfully of all the movies she'd seen in which anyone over the age of twelve could pick a lock with a hairpin. The big plastic clip holding her hair back would never do. She knew, though, that somewhere in the bowels of the huge handbag she had that other staple of the lockpicking tradition. She rummaged until she found a nail file and then poked at the lock. No good. *Guess I wasn't meant for a life of crime. The shed's probably empty anyway.* She started to walk away, but turned back and looked thoughtfully at the padlock, wondering why anyone would bother to lock an empty shed.

There was a single, small window on each side of the shed. Except for the narrow path leading to the door, the area was littered with piles of rotting lumber, rusty nails protruding at regular intervals. Tall weeds grew around and between scattered pieces of wood. She leaned forward, trying to determine if a snake was concealed in the weeds or lying on a sunny board just out of sight.

"It's not supposed to be easy," she said aloud, needing to hear the sound of a human voice.

"What's not?"

She spun around, more startled than if the imagined snake had emerged from the weeds and offered her an apple.

"Barney," she said, after the few seconds it took her to remember where she had seen that rotund figure before. "What're you doing here?"

"That's my shed," he said, letting an expressive lift of an eyebrow inquire what she was doing.

She told him about her conversation with Emma, and said, "I was trying to figure out what Mr. Pynchon might have seen. When I sat on his stool, I saw a glint of light. I followed it here." She watched Barney's face as she spoke, and could tell by his eyes he was giving thoughtful attention to her words. When her explanation was finished, she looked past his shoulder, through the tunnel of overhanging branches, and realized that further down the path there was another clearing. She remembered going over the map with Goodley.

"Is that the clearing where I found Robin Langley's body?"

Barney nodded solemnly.

She shivered inwardly. "That belong to you, too?"

"No. My land ends at the edge of the woods. That belongs to Emma Malich."

"And the road to Brad Wilson's place is just beyond where the trees start again?"

Another solemn nod.

"I knew it was close, but I didn't know there was another road back here. This one isn't on the map."

"No," Barney agreed. "This hasn't been used in years."

"I wonder if Mr. Pynchon could see that clearing from the flea market."

"Could you? When you were sitting there on his stool?"

She shook her head. "No. I could barely see as far as this shed."

He nodded, seemed ready to dismiss the subject and go back to his barbecue stand.

She stopped him. "Do you use the shed?"

"Not personally. I rent it out."

"To Mr. Pynchon?"

"Mm-hmm."

"So this is where he stores the books and records he offers for sale." She said this more to herself than to Barney.

"Yes," Barney said, confirming the contents of the shed. "He said it was easier for him than lugging those heavy books home every day."

"And if someone asked for something he didn't have with him, he might come down here in the middle of the day."

"He did that fairly often."

"Did he have a regular schedule?"

"Like a clock. He stopped at my place for coffee every morning by six, and then headed down to the shed to pick up whatever he was going to put out for sale that day. He was back setting up by seven."

"When did he take the unsold things back?"

"Depended on the crowd. Usually not until around three or maybe four o'clock."

"The day I was here, he told me he would look to see if he had any records like the ones I needed. Is this where he would have come to look?"

"Probably."

"Do you know what time he came here that day?"

"No." He laughed. "I'm pretty busy myself. No time to keep track of everybody else."

"You don't remember anything special about that day?"

He shook an admonishing finger at her. "You're beginning to sound like Goodley."

"God help me." She attempted to match his jocularity. "So Goodley knows about this road. And he's asked all these questions."

"Mm-hmm."

"Mind if I hang around a while? Just look around?"

"No," he said, adding, "Nice of you to ask."

She felt herself blush. "Sorry about that," she said, gesturing toward the shed she had been ready to break into.

After Barney left, she walked down the narrow road to the spot where she and Kate had left the car and, eventually, to where she had found her car and Robin's body.

The crime scene tape was still in place. She saw again that the road continued past where she had found the car. That meant that the meadow could be reached from three different directions: from the shed and the flea market, from Brad's house, and from whatever lay ahead. All she could see from her present vantage point was a barn that looked ready to collapse and beyond that, the road seemed to disappear behind a hill. She remembered the day she had borrowed Ellen's car to visit the crime scene and had noticed the direction in which weeds were crushed. The figure watching her from the woods had distracted her and she hadn't pursued this.

She looked around, forcing herself to remember details. She and

Kate had approached from the lane that went past Brad's house. When the lane ended, they turned left. The car was facing them. So, unless someone had driven down that road and turned the car around, an unlikely prospect, they must have come down the deserted road that ran along the river. *From the flea market? Doubt it.* The car was facing toward the flea market, not away from it. *However, the same road coming from the direction of the barn . . . Where does it lead?*

She followed the little-used road until she reached the barn. When she crested the hill, she saw it led to the highway to Memphis.

She walked back to the clearing and stood in the raised area between the car tracks where the maroon Taurus had been found.

"This was found in one of the tracks left by your car."

She could hear Goodley's words, could see his face clearly just before she had seen her bracelet in his hand. She saw, too, Goodley's careful examination of the area around the car that awful day when Robin's body had been discovered. The bracelet had not been present then. She knew she hadn't dropped it when she came back and had been observed by Brad from the tree line. As a matter of fact, Goodley even said it hadn't been there as recently as two days before their encounter the morning she had gone with Tom to retrieve the disabled rental car. So when did it get there? And how? Someone had to put it there. But why? Who? A personal possession of hers. How did they get it? A lot of questions. And no answer that didn't scare the daylights out of her.

Chapter Twenty-nine

Jennie hunched over the kitchen table, listing in a spiral notebook everything she could remember about Robin, particularly any encounters between Robin and Tom. She ignored the hollow feeling in her chest, even the rage that flamed and threatened to consume her. There would be time for that later. Now she had to be objective. The kids came first. No matter what happened, their world must be preserved. She wrote quickly, filling the page, turned to a fresh one, and wrote a similar account of everything she knew of the relationship between Robin and Web. The Barrons were a powerful family. How did they fit into this? Did they? Robin and Brad. She stopped writing as she remembered that night in the cabin, contrasting his anger then with his behavior at Riverview when Goodley had brought them together. Thank God he chose not to press charges. Why didn't he?

She felt the answer must be in the letters, if only she knew how to interpret them. Should she tell Goodley about them? How long would it take him to figure out about Tom and Robin if he read them? Did he already know? *I don't think so. If he did, he'd try to use it somehow. He's stumped. That's what this morning was all about. He was trying to make something happen. He didn't really care if Brad pressed charges against me.* She wondered what Goodley would do if he found out about the letters. Fortunately, the most damaging one was tucked safely away in the family Bible. She turned to another page in the notebook and wrote what she remembered of each letter.

He said he would rather see me dead than have me lose my immortal soul. What a chilling thing for a parent to say to a child. Had Joe meant it?

168

Emma. Had Robin been right that she would try to stop the marriage? Absolutely. No doubt about that. But how far would Emma go? Why didn't she like Robin? *She was friendly enough with me this morning. Started off a little rocky, but we ended up okay. She was actually helpful. Is she manipulating me?*

Web. Web's problem. *If you knew his mother, you'd understand.* After this morning, Jennie was pretty sure she understood the problem, but did it have anything to do with the murder? She doubted it. However, with a family like the Barronses, you never knew. Touchy. Maybe she could find a way to approach Leda.

Ellen. In some ways, that seemed the strangest of all. How did Ellen become involved? That seemed a good place to start. She lay her pen aside and reached for the phone.

"Hello." Her cousin sounded as brisk and no-nonsense as always.

"Hi, Ellen, it's me, Jennie."

A long silence.

"Ellen?"

"I'm glad you called. I was worried. Did you get the car fixed?"

"How'd you hear about that?"

"You know there are no secrets in this neighborhood."

She groaned inwardly, wondering exactly what was buzzing over the grapevine.

Ellen said, "You should have called me to come get you."

"I didn't want to do that."

"Don't lock me out, Jennie. We're family."

"I'm not locking you out. It's just—"

"Family's what you need now."

She glanced down at the spiral notebook, "Maybe you're right. There is something I'd like to talk to you about."

"What?"

"It's kind of involved. Actually, that's why I called."

"Oh?"

"Are you busy now?"

"No. Come on over."

Ellen greeted Jennie with a quick hug at the front door, and then led her into the immaculate living room. "What's this all about?"

Jennie countered with a question of her own. "How well did you know Robin?"

"You sound like Goodley."

"You're the second person who's said that to me today." Jennie wasn't sure how she felt about that. Something to think about later. "How well did you know her?" she asked again.

"You know what my relationship with Robin was. What are you really asking?"

"I heard Robin and Brad were planning to elope—"

Ellen finished the sentence for her. "And that I was going to help them."

"Were you?"

"Robin confided in me that she planned to run away with Brad and get married in New Orleans. She was concerned about her mother."

"Only her mother? What about her father?"

"Actually, he was the problem. Joe had made up his mind that Brad was no good and was dead set against Robin seeing him. She told her mother she wasn't going to break up with him, but she didn't tell her they were getting married. She felt bad about that, but she thought if Gladys didn't know anything, then Joe couldn't blame her."

Jennie thought about this before she asked, "What was your part?"

"Robin asked me to give Gladys a letter, explaining things."

"You agreed?"

"You sound surprised."

"I am."

"Really? You're the one person I thought would understand."

Jennie didn't see the connection at first. "You mean because of Tom and me?"

Ellen nodded.

"Tom and I didn't elope."

"You were married all of six weeks after you met. You think the family wasn't concerned?"

"But everyone else knew him before that, and they all liked him."

She realized how naïve she'd been. Now, she'd probably go slower. But nineteen is not a careful age.

"They knew him as my friend, not as a prospective husband for you. There's a big difference."

Jennie argued, still not ready to concede. "Mom kept saying what a big step marriage is, and Daddy went on like he always does, but they didn't try to stop me."

"And you've never wondered why?"

She thought back, trying to remember exactly what her parents had said, all the things she'd been too full of her own feelings to listen to. She looked at her cousin. "You smoothed the way for us?"

Ellen nodded.

"I guess I took a lot for granted."

Ellen didn't comment.

"Why?" Jennie asked.

"Don't forget. I introduced you. Tom went to the talent competition as my guest. And when he saw you on the stage, he was completely enthralled. It was like a fairy tale. Love at first sight is something we'd all like to believe in. And when you announced that you were getting married . . . immediately . . . the family was shocked. Naturally, they turned to me, since I was the one who knew Tom best."

"What'd you say?"

"I don't remember exactly. Something about what a nice guy he was, how I knew he'd take care of you. It doesn't matter now. It all worked out. Anyway, seeing Robin so determined to be with Brad reminded me of you back then. I guess she sensed somehow that I was sympathetic and she came to me for help."

"I never realized . . . I mean about you smoothing things over with the family. I was so in love . . . I guess I was oblivious." *And I stayed that way for eleven years.*

They sat quietly until Ellen said, "Okay, that's the story of how I got involved in Robin's plans. Your turn. Tell me how you happened to be brought home by the police the other night."

So Jennie told Ellen about the visit to Southern Lites, about entering Brad's house, the letters. She told her about the mysterious figure in the other car, her own car trouble. She even told her about Tom's little interlude with Robin. "I still can't believe it. The funny thing is . . . he swears he loves me . . . and I believe him."

"Even after . . . ?"

Jennie searched her cousin's face. "You don't think he does?"

Ellen rearranged the pillows on the sofa before she answered. "I can't help thinking . . . Robin was only a year younger than you were when he first saw you . . . and I remember how he was then. If anyone had tried to keep you apart . . ."

Jennie leaned forward, bringing her face within inches of Ellen's. "What're you saying?"

"You know how single-minded Tom is."

"So?"

"Just be careful."

She was stung by Ellen's words. She felt six years old again, being reprimanded by her adored older cousin, and responded defensively, "I am. I'm being very careful."

"Doesn't sound like it. You don't have any idea who followed you to Brad's house and disabled your car. And yet, you just keep running around like everything's normal."

"What do you expect me to do? Hibernate?"

"There's a big difference between hibernating and what you're doing. Ever heard of a happy medium?"

Jennie didn't answer.

Ellen asked, "Who knew you were going out there?"

Jennie shrugged.

Ellen said, "From what you've told me, Kate's the—"

"Don't start on Kate. You've never liked her. You've never liked any of my friends."

"That's not true. It's just that you have a tendency to trust too easily."

Jennie sensed a lecture coming and cut it off. "I have to go. It's time to pick up the kids."

"You're still not letting them ride the bus?"

"No."

"Aren't you being a little overprotective?"

"First I'm too trusting. Now I'm overprotective. Make up your mind."

Jennie glanced at her house as she approached and did a double take. *Tom's car is in the driveway. What's he doing home so early?* There was no time to check now. She had to be at school before the buses loaded. Her instructions had been explicit, but still, she was afraid if she wasn't there, the teachers might forget and let the kids ride the bus.

Chapter Thirty

Daddy! How come you're home?"

Tommy was right behind his brother, the same question in his eyes.

"I came home early to see my monkeys," Tom told them. "Maybe play a little soccer."

"Yes!" The two of them shouted in unison, too young, or maybe just too pleased with the prospect of a game with their father, to notice his restless pacing.

"How about you?" Tom looked at Jennie, spreading his arms, inviting her to join in the family embrace.

"Maybe a short game," she answered, declining to step forward. She watched from across the kitchen, speculating on possible reasons for her husband's agitation.

"What's up?" she asked Tom when they came back in after half an hour of spirited two-on-two. The boys were still outside, kicking the soccer ball around.

He didn't explain. Instead, he asked, "What are you trying to do?"

"About what? What do you mean?"

"Calling the office. Asking my secretary if I'm in. Hanging up before I get to the phone."

"I don't know what you're talking about."

His shoulders were rigid. He leaned forward a little. "You didn't call me?"

"I absolutely did not."

"Caller ID says you did."

It took Jennie a few minutes to realize what must have happened and a few seconds after that to understand how menacing the situation had become. She sat down and motioned for him to do the same. "There's something I didn't tell you," she said.

He looked wary. "Oh?"

"My cell phone's missing. That night out at Brad's . . . I know I left it in the car when I went into his house. When I got back, it was gone. That's why I had to walk to Southern Lites. I couldn't call for help."

He put his elbows on the table and buried his face in his hands. When he looked up, he asked, "Did you tell the police?"

"No."

"Jeez! Why not?"

"I don't know. With everything that happened . . . I guess I forgot." She paused to watch Tommy and Andy sprawled on their backs in the grass. She looked at Tom. "Is that why you came home early? Because of a phone call?"

"More than a phone call. It seemed like every five minutes, the phone rang and someone asked for me. We were in a meeting to work out a marketing strategy for the new software package and we couldn't get anything done. Finally, I said I had to leave. See if I could find out what the problem was."

"I don't understand. Don't you usually turn your cell off for those meetings?"

"The calls were to my office phone."

"I never call that number."

"I know. That's why I thought . . ."

Jennie felt like firecrackers were going off inside her head. "Thought what? That I was deliberately trying to make trouble? That I was acting like a jealous wife?"

"I didn't say that."

"You may as well have."

He reached across the table. "I love you, Jennie. Since the first time I saw you, I've never, even for one second, loved anyone else."

She moved her hand beyond his reach. "Don't say that to me. Not now."

"It's true."

"Maybe so, but—"

"No buts, Jennie. We're what's important. Our family. All this other . . . I'll probably never be able to make you understand how sorry I am . . . we can't let it drive us apart." He gestured toward the window. Tommy and Andy were still sprawled in the grass. "What about them?"

"That's not fair."

"Sorry."

"Forget sorry. Let's get back to the issue. I didn't call your office today. Somebody stole my phone. Whoever did made those calls." After a moment, she asked, "You didn't recognize the voice?"

"I told you. I never talked to the person. They always hung up before I got on the line."

"And you thought it was me?"

"What was I supposed to think?"

"Marge knows my voice. Did she think it was me?"

"She said the signal was bad. It kept breaking up. I got worried. Afraid you'd gone out to that house again."

"Give me a little credit. I have better sense than that. I did go up to River County though." She told him how she'd spent her day: the white station wagon behind the dumpster in the school parking lot, the confrontation at Riverview, her visit to Emma, her exploration of the road running along the river and, finally, her visit to Ellen.

By the time she finished, Tom's tan had faded to a chalky white. "You shouldn't have gone to the flea market. Not alone. What if Brad had been there? After breaking into his house—"

"It wasn't the house he was mad about. It was more the letters—"

"Letters?"

Too late, she remembered she hadn't intended to tell him about the letters. Now . . . Not much choice. *Oh well, it'll be interesting to see his reaction.* "There were some letters in a box. They were from Robin. I was reading them when he came home."

"No wonder he was mad."

"I know. But he didn't seem like he was bent on revenge or anything."

"What did the letters say?" Tom was pacing again. "Did she mention me?"

Jennie nodded.

"What'd she say?"

"I don't remember specifically."

"That doesn't seem like something you'd forget."

"I didn't mean I forgot. Her references to you weren't very specific . . . something about 'after what happened with Tom' . . . no, actually, she mentioned you by your initials, but of course I knew."

He looked away.

"Did you know Robin was going to marry Brad?"

"No."

She couldn't tell how he felt about this. There was no clue in his voice, no change in his expression. "Ellen knew," she said, probing.

"Ellen?"

Jennie nodded. "She thinks your attraction to Robin was like your attraction to me, back when—"

"That's insane!"

"Maybe, but back to the letters—it seems everyone was against Brad and Robin being together."

"Well, I know Joe and Gladys—"

"Apparently, Gladys didn't mind all that much, but Joe . . ." Jennie paused, remembering what Robin's note had said about him. "And Emma. She was dead set against it."

"Who's Emma?"

"Friend of Brad's, an older lady. A real piece of work. She owns the house he lives in."

"What does she have to do with this?"

"Seems like she kind of adopted Brad. Emotionally, I mean. She thinks everything's my fault. Anyway, that's what she said. And something about Edward trying to protect me."

"Who's Edward?"

"Mr. Pynchon, the record dealer. Remember? He's the guy who had the accident. Apparently he knows something."

"That's in the letters too?"

"No. Emma told me that."

"Jeez, I feel like I need a program." He actually looked amused. It didn't last long. "Where are the letters?"

"The last time I saw them they were scattered all over Brad's floor."

"Goodley know about them?"

"I don't think so." The letters were not the foremost thing on Jennie's mind. "I'm scared for the kids. Someone's watching them. Following them. Goodley doesn't believe me, but I know I'm right."

"What would anyone—"

"You don't believe me either."

"Actually, no, because it doesn't make sense."

"The phone calls to your office must be related." She looked at her watch. "It's not quite five. Why don't you check with Marge? See if there were more calls after you left."

In the brief moment before the phone was answered, they stared out the window, watching their sons. Andy picked up a stick, pointed it at his brother, who clutched his chest and fell to the ground, feigning death. Jennie continued to watch as she listened to Tom's side of the phone conversation.

"Well?" she said after he placed the receiver back in its cradle.

"There were two more calls. One about five minutes after I left. Another fifteen minutes after that. Then nothing."

"And it takes you about twenty-five minutes to drive home."

He nodded. "More or less, probably a little less today since it was before rush hour."

She was thinking about this, trying to determine what it meant, when she realized Tom was talking to her.

"So? How about it?" he said.

"How about what?"

"I knew you weren't listening."

She forced herself to pay attention. "What'd you say?"

"I think we should go away for a week. Just the two of us. Take some time—"

"I can't do that! What about the kids?"

Tom opened his mouth.

"It's not open for discussion," Jennie said, before he could begin again.

"All right. All right." He turned away, began to pace, stalking to one corner of the room before he turned sharply to the next. "We'll take them with us."

"Impossible. They have school. What about my job? Your job?"

"Those things can wait."

She put her hands to her ears. "Don't! I said I won't go and I won't! I can't."

"Are you afraid of me, Jennie?"

Chapter Thirty-one

Unable to sleep, Jennie spent the night trying to figure out the significance of Robin's letters. One line in particular niggled at her. Had Joe really said he would rather see his daughter dead than have her lose her immortal soul? Did he believe her relationship with Brad was causing that to happen? How far would he go to stop the relationship? By the time dawn filtered through the blinds, she had come to a decision. Awkward though it would be, she had to confront Joe. What would it accomplish? Maybe nothing. If so, she would move on to other people mentioned in the letters. With the safety of Tommy and Andy at stake, she wasn't about to sit around and wait for Goodley to find the killer.

She arrived at Riverview early and went first to the chaplain's office. As usual, the door was open. The chair behind the desk was turned toward the window, with just the top of an iron-gray head visible above its back. Jennie tapped on the door frame. "Got a minute?" she asked when Joe swiveled to face her.

"Sure."

She entered the room and settled herself across from him. Unsure how to begin, she pointed to the display of framed photographs occupying one corner of an otherwise uncluttered desk and said, "Robin was a beautiful girl."

Joe selected a picture and handed it to Jennie. "This one's my favorite." It was a snapshot of himself, some years ago, resplendent in his dress uniform, with Robin, at about age five, sitting on his lap, wearing his hat and grinning from ear to ear.

She studied the photo and replaced it gently on the desk. "Joe, I know it's hard for you to talk about . . . everything . . . right now, but there's something I need to ask you." She steeled herself and went on. "I read some letters Robin wrote to Brad shortly before she died and—"

"Do you have them?" The question came out like whiplash.

It caught her off guard. "The letters? No." Unable to think of any other alternative, she told him about her uninvited visit to Brad's home, ending with, "I'd like this to remain confidential."

He spread his hands impatiently. "What did they say?"

"I didn't have a chance to read much. Brad came home . . . and I had to get out of there fast."

"He threatened you?"

"No, I can't honestly say he threatened me."

Joe was watching her with half-closed eyes, fingering the wooden crucifix he always wore. "Tell me about the letters."

"They were love letters." She winced at the pain that crossed his features. *Don't ask questions if you don't want the answer.* "She did love him, Joe."

No comment on that. Instead, he said, "You had a question."

She rephrased the question she'd come to ask. "I wondered if you and Gladys knew Brad very well."

Instead of answering, he swiveled the chair so that his face was hidden from her. When he turned back, he asked, "Do you have them?"

"No."

There was a long moment of silence, more fingering of the crucifix. Finally, he said, "Surely you understand how much anything that concerns our daughter would mean to Gladys and me."

"If I had them, I'd give them to you."

She knew he didn't believe her.

After Jennie left Joe's, she had a planning session with the psychologist who was advising her on programs for the residents. The meeting lasted over an hour. When it was over, she went directly to the small room used as an office by Leda Barrons, the Director of Volunteer Services. She smoothed her skirt and brushed her hair back with her fingers before she knocked.

"Jennifer. How nice. I rarely see you now that you're a member of the staff. Tell me, are you happy with your new position?"

She's acting like the scene in the dining hall didn't happen. "It's been hectic with everything else that's going on, but it's fine." Jennie lifted her chin and continued, "I've come to talk to you about something else." She stepped the rest of the way into the room and closed the door behind her. "I read some letters that Robin wrote shortly before her death."

Leda leaned forward, her manner elaborately casual. "The letters you talked to Joe about?"

Jennie nodded, a little surprised that Joe had told Leda about the letters. She said, "Robin mentioned something about Web's problem."

"Quite possibly the problem was hers. Not Webster's." There was a definite coolness in Leda's manner now.

Jennie barreled ahead anyway. "Last Friday, when we were all in the dining hall . . . it was pretty obvious he'd been drinking."

The coolness became ice. "Gentlemen do that sometimes."

"Not at nine-thirty in the morning. And Web's only eighteen."

Leda stood, drawing her short body to its full height. "I have no intention of discussing my son with you"—she waved one scarlet-tipped finger—"and you will not discuss my son with anyone else. Do you understand?"

"I'm just trying—"

"Very well. Give me the letters and I will discuss the matter with Web."

"I don't have them."

"I have every right to see them if they concern my son."

"I told you. I don't have them."

Leda looked skeptical, as if she didn't know what to say, but only for a second. She said, "Riverview depends in large part on the efforts of volunteers. And on charitable gifts"—Leda paused, raising an eyebrow on the last two words—"to raise this institution above the level of those unfortunate places one reads about from time to time."

"I know that."

"Please don't interrupt. It has occurred to me, and I feel certain I'm not the only one, that your involvement in this scandal, unsavory at best, might cause some of our benefactors to think carefully before making gifts in the future."

"None of the things that happened were my fault." *Why am I defending myself?* "I came to you hoping—"

Leda cut her off. "I think it's time for you to report for your duties."

Jennie spent the rest of the day playing catch up for the time spent with Joe and Leda, leaving her no time to visit Pynchon in the East Wing.

As she drove home, turning the two conversations over in her mind, she was still a little surprised that Joe had told Leda about the letters after she had asked him to keep the information confidential. She was trying to sort it out in her head when she walked in the kitchen and found Tom, still in his suit, talking on the phone. He hung up just as she came in.

"You're early again," she said, bending to pick up Smokey. She felt the cat's nervous tension and wondered what had upset him. She turned to Tom. "More phone calls?"

He nodded. "I called Goodley. Told him about the calls and that your phone was missing."

"What did he say?"

"Not much. Now that he knows, he can track down the location of the tower that transmitted the signals."

"That means?"

"It'll tell him the location from which the calls were made."

This conversation was carried on as they walked down the hall toward their bedroom.

"Oh, my God!" The sight that greeted her almost caused Jennie's knees to buckle. The room was in shambles. Drawers had been removed from her dresser and piled on the bed. Her belongings were scattered throughout the room. White-faced, she spun around to face Tom. "What happened?"

"I don't know. I just got home."

"Someone's looking for the letters."

"You said you don't have them."

"Looks like somebody thinks I do."

She looked at Tom's dresser, which had not been touched, and then at him. "Why didn't you tell me?"

"Tell you what?"

"About this." She waved her hand above the disheveled piles.

"I didn't know."

"How could you not know?"

"I told you I just got home. I stopped to call the office from the phone in the kitchen. I didn't come in here until now."

She sat on the bed, fighting nausea, careful not to touch any of the tainted garments.

"Jennie, I didn't know. I just got home."

"I'd better call Goodley." She picked up the phone and then put it back, shaking her head. "I can't."

"Why not?"

"He'd ask a lot of questions, like why anyone would do this."

"Don't you want to know?"

"It's the letters. Everyone wants them."

"Where are they?"

"I don't have them."

"Then why does everyone think you do?"

She ignored the question. "I didn't tell Goodley about them. If he finds out now—"

"Who did you tell?"

"Just about everybody except Goodley." She remembered her conversations with Joe and Leda. Thinking back, she knew she hadn't seen either of them after lunch. They were both in positions where they set their own schedules and could have left at any time during the afternoon. They both knew where she lived. Who else had she told? Ellen. Kate. Both of them knew she kept a spare key under a flowerpot by the front door. Neither Joe nor Leda did, but it wouldn't take much imagination to look for one there.

Tom put his hand on her arm. "Don't try to do this alone. Let me help you."

She moved away from his touch and looked at him, wondering if he could be responsible for the scene before them. She knew he desperately wanted to read the letters, but would he violate their home in this way? She didn't want to believe he would. They stood on opposite sides of the bed watching each other.

He broke the silence. "We need to get away."

"Don't start that again. You know I can't."

"We'll take the kids. Keep them safe with us."

At the mention of the children, Jennie glanced at the clock. "It's time to pick them up." She turned to leave, and then stopped. "You get them today. I'll take care of this."

After he was gone, she stood for a moment looking around. The drawers from her dresser made a shaky tower in the center of the bed. Her things were scattered over the floor; a lacy camisole lay alone in a corner. Nothing belonging to Tom had been displaced.

Chapter Thirty-two

The next morning Tom suggested again they get away for a few days. "Come on, Jen. At least think about it."

"No. I've told you a dozen times I won't. I can't." She heard the boys moving around in their room and wondered, *Are they safe here?*

Andy came into the kitchen. "What can't you do, Mom?"

"This is something between Daddy and me. Cheerios or cornflakes?"

"Cornflakes."

"Tommy," she called, "cornflakes okay with you?"

"Yeah."

She stopped midway in her reach into the cabinet. "He sounds hoarse."

Tom pointed out that he'd only said one word, and not much of a word at that.

"You feel all right?" she asked when Tommy joined them in the kitchen. She kissed his forehead, testing his temperature the old-fashioned way. No fever. "Does your throat feel scratchy?"

He shook his head.

"I think you better stay home."

"I can't. We're doing multiplication tables."

"You'll be doing multiplication tables all the time now."

"This is different. It's a contest. The principal's gonna visit our class and watch while we do flash cards."

"I'm sure she'll come again."

"But I'm the best one. I'll get my name on the bulletin board in the main hall."

186

"It's a nice day. He wouldn't stay in bed if he did stay home." Tom was not making this easy.

Did he want everyone out of the house? She said, "It's supposed to rain later."

"Oh, what do those guys know? They're wrong more often than they're right."

"Yeah, Mom, those guys are never right." Tommy agreed with his father and flashed him a grateful smile.

Andy put his two cents in. "That's right, Mom. Those guys don't know anything."

Jennie looked at the three faces turned toward her and threw up her hands. She turned to Tommy. "If your throat starts to feel scratchy, even a little bit, have the nurse call me."

Driving to work, she looked at the brilliant sky and told herself Tommy hadn't sounded that bad.

During a long, sleepless night, she'd decided neither Joe nor Leda could be guilty of the break-in. True, each of them wanted to read the letters, but both had too much confidence in their powers of persuasion to resort to such tactics. Not wanting to have to withstand any pressure they might bring to bear, she avoided them all morning. She finished the morning sing-along and hurried to the East Wing without stopping for lunch.

Perfect, she thought when she saw the vacant plastic chair by the door of Room E46. A quick check revealed Edward Pynchon alone in his room. He no longer had the large oxygen tank near his bed, nor was he connected to the network of tubes. His face was turned toward the window, so Jennie couldn't tell if his eyes were open. She closed the door behind her as quietly as she could and tiptoed to the bed. Asleep. *Should I wake him? I have to,* she thought. *He's the only one who knows. Will he remember?*

"Mr. Pynchon, Edward," she said softly. When he didn't respond, she touched his shoulder lightly and repeated his name. He opened his eyes, seemed to look at her, pointed to the water carafe, and put his fingers to his lips. She wasn't sure if he recognized her. "Can you talk?" she asked.

There was a soft sound, not a recognizable word.

When she leaned forward, the light from the window illuminated her face. There was a sharp intake of breath from the figure on the bed.

He *does* know me.

She poured water into a glass and helped him to a semi-sitting position. In the hall outside she heard the creak of a wheelchair, followed by footsteps muffled by rubber-soled shoes and the hum of idle conversation.

"Are you afraid of me?" she asked, easing his head back to the pillow.

He shook his head.

"Do you trust me?"

There was a slight movement of the muscles around his mouth. An attempted smile, she hoped.

"I want to talk to you for a few minutes," she told him, "if it's not too much for you."

"Been waiting for you," he said.

She smiled, encouraging him. "You saw something, didn't you?"

He nodded.

"Can you tell me what it was?"

"The television." He paused, seemed confused, and then continued. "The funeral . . . you and your family . . . you look . . ." His voice trailed off.

"How did I look?"

He hesitated, seemed to be listening to the hum of voices in the hall.

Jennie tried to regain his attention. "Have you told the police what you saw?"

He shook his head. "I wanted to warn you first."

The hum of voices stopped abruptly, replaced by footsteps not made by soft-soled shoes. "Warn me about what?" Jennie whispered as the heavy footsteps came closer.

He put a finger to his lips.

Goodley came bursting through the door. "What're you doing in here?" He looked from Jennie to the figure on the bed. "Did he talk to you?"

The old man took hold of Jennie's hand and squeezed it softly.

She acknowledged his signal by an equally soft pressure on his fingers, and did not answer Goodley's question.

Goodley turned to the orderly who had come in with him. "Has he talked yet?"

The orderly shook his head.

Goodley studied the chart at the foot of the bed. "What's this mumbo jumbo anyway?"

"Trauma to the head. If you want any more information you'll have to talk to the doctor."

An aide came in with a tray.

"Let me take that," Jennie offered. "I'll give him his lunch."

The aide said, "He's been feeding himself."

"It seems the only thing he can't do is talk," Goodley said peevishly.

The aide placed the tray on the wheeled table by Pynchon's bed and adjusted it for him. The old man gave Jennie a sly smile and picked up his fork, ignoring Goodley and the others in the room.

Jennie said, "Okay if I stay here and keep him company?"

"Excellent idea." Goodley pulled a chair closer to the bed and sat down. "I'll join you."

Pynchon spilled apple juice into his plate.

"Now look what you've done." The aide was visibly annoyed. "Not you, dear," she said to the patient. "Don't worry about it. I'll get another tray." She turned to Goodley. "You've upset him. You always do. You'll have to go." And, to Jennie, "You too."

Jennie left without argument, knowing Pynchon wouldn't talk to her with Goodley in the room. She'd come back later—alone—and find out why. The policeman caught up with her in the hall and said, "I'd like to talk to you."

She glanced at her watch. "I only have a few minutes. Wednesday afternoons we play bingo."

"This won't take long."

She led him into the recreation area, a bright, pleasant room with large picture windows overlooking the landscaped courtyard. A pair of massive oaks framed the view. Branches moved restlessly, seeming to beckon the clouds beginning to gather on the horizon. "I have to set up for the bingo game. Okay if I work while we talk?"

"When's the last time you used your cell phone?"

"I don't know about the last call. The last time I know I had the phone was just before I went into Brad's house."

"You're sure?"

"Positive." There was an incisive snap as she lay each card on the table.

Goodley watched her without comment.

"You don't believe me?"

"The nature of the calls . . ." He finished with an expressive shrug.

"You mean like a wife who's checking up on her husband?"

He left a silence for her to fill.

"I don't do that. Check up on Tom, I mean. Besides, you should know I couldn't have made the calls."

"Why?"

"Tom said they started Friday morning. About the time we—you, Brad, Emma, me—we were all here at Riverview. Remember? It was the day you tried to get Brad to press charges against me."

Goodley's phone rang and he stepped out into the hall to answer it.

Residents began drifting in, greeting and teasing each other as they seated themselves at the tables Jennie had set up for the bingo game. Some brought pictures of grandchildren to share with her. With Goodley out in the hall, still talking on the phone, her responses this morning were less enthusiastic than usual, but apparently enough to satisfy the residents.

"G34," she called, keeping one eye on Goodley. She let out a relieved sigh when he hurried away. *Maybe I'm off the hook.*

By the time she left at two o'clock, the sky looked as if the weatherman might be smarter than Tom and the kids thought. She hoped the storm would hold off at least a little longer, but a low rumbling warned her it wouldn't. She was getting into her car, thinking of Tommy's throat, when she heard Goodley's irritating, nasal voice.

"Mrs. Connors."

"I thought you left hours ago."

"I came back. It looks like the calls originated in the vicinity of your house." Before she had time to respond, he asked, "Is there anything you want to tell me?"

Jennie inhaled deeply, blew out the air. "I already told you. My phone was stolen the night I went out to Brad's house."

"That was last Wednesday, a week ago."

"Right."

"Your husband reported it just yesterday. Why didn't you tell me?" He stepped closer. "You've had plenty of opportunities. A whole week."

She forced herself to meet his gaze. "I don't know why I didn't tell you."

"I checked with the phone company. Apparently you didn't report it to them either."

"I guess I forgot."

He took another step forward, looming over her. "How could you forget?"

She resisted the urge to step back. "With everything that's happened . . ." A large, fat raindrop landed on Jennie's cheek when she looked up into Goodley's face. "I have to pick up my kids. I'm sure whoever messed with my car took my phone. And I've already told you everything I can about that." She turned to leave.

"One more thing, Mrs. Connors."

"What?" More raindrops hit her face. She resisted the urge to bolt.

"I understand you're taking a trip."

"Who told you that?"

"Mr. Connors."

"We're not going anywhere. Please. I have to pick up my kids."

The rain was falling harder.

"Did you make those phone calls?"

"No. I was with you Friday morning. You know that."

"I checked the exact times of the calls. You could have made them from the car before and after seeing me."

"But I didn't. May I go? The kids are waiting."

When he did not object, she turned to leave.

"Mrs. Connors," he called, as she was opening the car door, "if you do decide to go away, don't go far." His words echoed in her head as she drove toward the school.

She dashed through the rain to the school's entrance and went directly to the room where the children usually waited. They weren't there. A janitor was taking a pail from a closet. "Afternoon, Mrs. Connors," he said.

"Have you seen my children?"

"Seems like I saw them get on the bus."

"But I've been picking them up."

He shrugged.

She raced down the hall to the principal's office. The door was closed. She knocked, then pushed the door open. A meeting was in progress. She didn't care. "Where are my children?"

"You weren't here so I told them to ride the bus."

"But I told you I'd be picking them up."

"I assumed because it was raining you decided—"

Jennie left without waiting for her to finish. By the time she pulled out of the parking lot, the rain was coming down in a solid sheet, blowing against her windshield so hard the wipers couldn't keep up.

"They'll be soaked. Tommy'll wind up with strep throat." She talked to herself as she drove, voicing the least of the fears that crowded her mind. "Almost there," she said when she passed the stone gates that marked the entrance to her neighborhood, Rolling Hills. She saw the green truck as she turned onto their street.

Chapter Thirty-three

Jennie stopped the car before she reached the garage and ran to the front door. *Don't panic.* The old mantra played in her head. *It's okay. They know where the spare key is. They can let themselves in.* She turned the knob. *Locked. Doesn't mean they're not here. Don't panic. I always tell them, if they have to use that key, go inside and lock the door behind you.*

She was shaking so hard she had to use one hand to steady the other to fit her key into the lock. It seemed to take an eternity.

"Hey, guys, I'm home."

No response. She went first to the family room. Empty. The TV screen was blank.

"Tommy, Andy, it's me. I'm home."

Still no response.

She stepped back outside and looked under the flowerpot. *The key's gone. Maybe they went in and couldn't find me, so they went next door.* She ran across the lawn and rang Kate's doorbell. That stillness could only come from an empty house. She looked around, fighting to remain calm. *The green truck. It's still here.*

The torrential downpour had settled into a steady rain that fell in straight, unrelenting lines, pelting the street. She ran toward the truck, too scared to be surprised when the driver rolled down the window as she approached.

"My children," she shouted, holding onto the vehicle's door and peering inside. She gulped and forced herself to speak slowly. "Two boys. Six and eight." She craned her neck, trying to see past him. The rain ran down her face, into her eyes as she strained to see through the window into the back of the truck. "Have you seen them?"

193

"A lady picked them up when they got off the bus. She took them there." He pointed toward Ellen's house.

She ran up the street and, when she reached Ellen's, pounded on the door, her hands too shaky to manage the bell.

It was Andy who came to the door. "You're right, Aunt Ellen, it's Mom."

Jennie reached forward and gathered him in her arms.

"Where were you?" Tommy demanded, coming into the foyer behind his brother.

Unable to speak, she extended her other arm, including Tommy in the embrace.

"Thank God you're safe." She bent to kiss each of them.

Tommy pulled away. "You're all wet."

"Are you cold, Mom?" Andy asked.

She couldn't control the tremors. "No, I'm just . . . just so glad to see you."

Ellen joined them in the foyer. "You should get out of those clothes."

Jennie looked down at the water on the floor and realized how wet she was. Her sweater and slacks clung to her. She was shivering, but did not feel cold. Tears, warm and salty, mingled with the rain on her face. She looked at her sons. The fronts of their shirts were soaked where she'd held them against her, but they were safe. She laughed and said, "You're safe," giddy with the realization that, for the moment at least, it was true.

Ellen, as usual, took charge. "I'll get a robe. Make you something hot to drink."

Jennie shook her head. "I just want to get home."

"It's pouring out there."

"We have only half a block to go." She held the sweater away from her body. "I can't get any wetter than I already am. Just let me have an umbrella for them."

Ellen hesitated, studying Jennie's face. Finally, she moved to the stand in the corner. "Promise you'll call me later." She selected an oversized, black umbrella. "This should cover both of them."

In the moment it took Ellen to get the umbrella, Jennie's mind began to function. "Why are they here? The kids, I mean."

"I went to meet Elizabeth because of the rain. Tommy and Andy got off the bus too. You weren't there . . . it was raining hard."

"Thanks. You scared me to death but, thanks."

"I called the house. Left a message on your machine."

"The machine. I didn't even think to check."

Ellen opened her mouth, looked ready to speak. She glanced toward the boys, hesitated. "Why don't you two go back and finish watching that program with Elizabeth."

Jennie felt the fear rise in her throat. "Go on," she said to her children. She waited until they were out of earshot. "What is it?"

"As I said, I went to meet Elizabeth. The green truck was there. I wondered if it could be the one you told me about. Then I saw Tommy and Andy get off the bus. I was surprised, but I figured you'd been delayed, so I told them to come home with me."

"Thanks. I was petrified when I got to school and they were gone. Then I got home and they weren't there." Jennie shuddered. "I saw the truck."

"He's still there?"

"Yeah. He's the one who told me the kids were here."

"Down by the bus stop?" Ellen asked.

"No. About halfway between your house and mine. At least that's where he was a few minutes ago."

"Is it the truck you told me about?"

"Yes." Jennie moved into living room and stood beside the window. "He hasn't moved." She tried to make out the number on the license plate, but it was raining too hard and the truck was too far away. If only she'd thought to look before, but all she could think of then was getting to Ellen's to see if the kids were really there. She went to the door of the family room. "Tommy, come here, please."

"In a minute."

"Now!"

"But Mom."

"I said now, Thomas."

The child joined his mother and Ellen, dragging his feet and grumbling. "I'm gonna miss the best part."

Jennie put her hand on his shoulder, directed him to the window, and pointed to the truck. "Is that the man who took the picture of you?"

"Tommy," Andy called from the other room. "Hurry. He's almost there!"

Tommy started to leave.

Jennie held him. "Is it the same man?"

"I guess so. I can't really see him from here."

She let go of Tommy's arm and stood watching the truck, thinking hard. The man had seemed . . . What? The ghost of an idea began to take shape in her head.

Tommy turned, and collided with his brother, who taunted him: "You missed it! That guy had the biggest gun I ever saw and . . ."

"I told you I was gonna miss the best part," Tommy said to his mother.

But her thoughts were not on the television show. "I'll do it," she said softly.

"Do what?" Ellen asked.

"Tom wanted to go away. I said no, but I changed my mind. I think it's the best way to handle this."

Ellen grabbed Jennie's arm. "What're you talking about?"

Jennie shook her off. "It's too complicated to explain right now."

"Jennie."

"I'll tell you later. Really, I will. Listen, thanks again for rescuing the kids. We have to go." She turned to her sons. "Zip your jackets."

Tommy pointed out, "You don't even have a jacket."

"I'll probably get sick. And you guys will have to take care of me." She feigned a lightness she did not feel.

"Yeah, we'll make you stay in bed and eat soup," Andy threatened.

Ellen was standing between Jennie and the door. "You're not going to do anything rash?"

Jennie waved the question away.

"You're sure you don't want my raincoat?" Ellen offered.

"Why bother?" Jennie held the wet sweater away from her body and wrung more water from it. "Sorry," she said, looking at the puddle on the usually gleaming marble tile.

The green truck was still there. She looked at her sons: two pairs of short legs beneath the black umbrella, marching on the pavement, which seemed to boil as the rain pounded. The umbrella tipped when they passed the truck.

Andy waved.

The driver waved back, and smiled at the kids.

Jennie looked at the license plate, but the number was obscured by spatters of mud. She looked at the driver, memorizing his face: long and narrow; prominent chin; hawk nose; a red baseball cap on his head, turned backward. Tufts of hair protruded from an opening in the cap. Not the bald guy. It's the other one. The man ducked his chin and turned away. She realized he was talking into a phone. She was beginning to think of the murder in a different way—a way that threatened the very foundation of her life.

She waited until everyone was served and the food had produced the customary lull around the dinner table. "I've changed my mind. Maybe we should go away for a few days. All of us."

Tom's expression was hard to read.

Tommy was instantly alert. "Away? Where?" he asked.

Andy was busy making sure no carrots touched his mashed potatoes and wasn't listening.

Tommy persisted. "Where are we going?"

"Going?" Andy looked up, holding the vegetables at bay with his fork.

"We're gonna take a trip," Tommy explained to his brother. He looked from one parent to the other and asked again, "Where?"

Tom answered, "We haven't decided yet."

Andy said, "How about Disney World?"

"Nothing like that," said Jennie.

Tom said, "How about the hunting camp?"

"That place of your uncle's?" Jennie said. "It's in the middle of nowhere."

"That's why it's perfect."

Perfect for what? A disturbing picture was becoming more and more clear in her head. One thing she still felt sure of, though, was that she and the kids would be safe with Tom.

Later, when the boys were in bed, she said, "Goodley said you told him we were going away. After I'd said, very clearly I think, that I wouldn't."

"I knew you'd change your mind."

She let that ride for the moment. "What made you think of the hunting camp?"

"I don't know. It's a place to get away from everything. Isn't that the idea?"

"It's pretty remote."

"Not really. It's just a little north of Barney's, and you didn't think twice about driving up there to shop."

"I'm not talking about distance. I mean isolated. No one around. Just the river and the woods."

Chapter Thirty-four

*F**riday. That's tomorrow. Doesn't give me much time. Tom's right, though. If we're going, the sooner the better. Still, there's not enough time. Waiting period.* She stared at a hummingbird floating outside the kitchen window. Doubts and plans jostled for position in her mind. *Have to borrow Dad's. Might be better anyway. Probably won't have to use it. Don't want one around after this is over. This way, Goodley . . . Could he stop me? Who knows?*

She pushed these thoughts aside and forced herself to concentrate on the spiral notebook. She reached for the phone, made the first of the listed calls, spoke briefly, drew a line, and dialed the next number.

So her morning went until it was time to leave for Riverview. There she went directly to Leda Barron's office. She hesitated before knocking on the volunteer director's door. *Be humble.*

Leda acknowledged Jennie's presence with a frosty smile and a slight inclination of her perfectly coifed head.

Jennie said, "I'm sorry if I upset you the other day."

The smile remained in place.

Jennie squared her shoulders. *Humility* "I've come to ask for your help." She gave Leda a moment to gloat. "I won't be here next week. Can one of your volunteers fill in for me? I've planned the activities." She held out two typewritten pages. "Here's a schedule."

Leda read through the list. "Very thorough. I'm sure I can find someone. When are you leaving?"

"Tomorrow evening. As soon as Tom gets home from work."

"You'll be gone how long?"

"A week. So it'll just be three days that I need a substitute, Tuesday, Wednesday, and Thursday of next week." She was aware of the

199

older woman's appraising scrutiny as she continued, "I'm hoping that by the time we get back, this mess will be settled and we can all get on with our lives."

"That would be nice."

Jennie herded the boys toward the car. "Andy, you carry the cat food and Smokey's toys. Tommy, you can hold Smokey in the picnic basket on your lap. Keep talking to him while the car is moving. A nice soft voice. You know what he likes."

"Does Grandma know we're coming?"

"Of course."

"Did you tell her we're going on a trip?"

"Yes, I did."

"I bet she made brownies for us to take along."

"I wouldn't be surprised."

Andy was right. Jennie's mother had spent the day baking. While she presented the cookies to her grandsons, Jennie went with her father into his study.

"You're sure you know how to use this?"

"You're the one who taught me."

"But so long ago."

"You don't forget something like that."

"You never were very good."

"I wasn't that bad," Jennie protested. "I don't really expect to need it. I'm just being extra careful."

"A gun in the hands of someone—"

"I know. I've given this a lot of thought." She showed her father that she remembered how to aim and shoot.

"The safety?"

She pointed to the appropriate small latch.

"Remember how to load?"

"Mm-hmm."

He unlocked the drawer where he kept the ammunition.

"Never mind, Dad. I know how." She demonstrated with the empty revolver.

"And I never thought you listened to anything I said."

Jennie felt a pang of regret. "Was I that bad?"

"No worse than most." The doting expression in his eyes negated the gruff words. He held out a small, rectangular box.

She shook her head. "No. I'll buy some tomorrow. Just tell me the best place."

"You're being very silly."

She treated him to her best Daddy's-girl smile. "I want to buy the ammunition myself."

"Why?"

Busying herself with the gun, she avoided the question.

"Will you have time?"

"I have all day tomorrow. Tom'll be at work and the kids at school." She slipped the gun in her purse while her father wrote down the name of a gun shop.

Jennie looked up the number of the gun shop and called ahead to make sure they carried the special ammunition she needed. Despite the assurances to her father, she was relieved when the owner suggested that she bring the gun along so he could go over the correct loading procedure with her. She spent more time with him than she had anticipated and just had time to stop at the grocery store before she picked up Tommy and Andy.

"Okay, guys, we have four bags. Help me get one in each arm. That's good. Now, if you each carry one, we can make it in one trip and—"

Tommy finished for her. "And we can start getting ready to go sooner."

"Right."

She was busy sorting and putting away groceries when she realized the patchwork bag was still in the car. "My purse." She slapped her forehead with the heel of her hand.

"I'll get it." Andy was out the door before she could protest.

"This thing weighs a ton, Mom. You got a brick in here?" he asked when he came back, and started to look into the bag.

"Andrew! No!"

The little boy was so startled by the intensity of her reaction that he dropped the purse on the floor with a thud.

"Sure sounds like a brick," Tommy said.

Andy was looking at his mother's face.

She picked up her purse and placed it securely on the back of the counter. "I've told you a million times not to look into ladies' purses."

"I just wanted to see what's so heavy."

"I carry a lot of things."

"I don't see what's the big deal about ladies' purses."

"They're private. It's not polite to look into them."

"What if I need a tissue?"

"Ask permission first. Enough about that. I've already packed your clothes. I want you to each pick out one game and one indoor toy."

"We won't have time for toys. Dad's gonna take us fishing."

"We might get more rain."

As soon as the boys were out of the kitchen, she checked the gun. *Everything looks okay. Safety's still on. Guess I should find another place to put it though. Where?* She finally decided on the small bag that held her personal items.

By the time they pulled out of the driveway and headed north, it was dark, and a slow, steady rain had begun to fall. The boys soon fell asleep. Jennie lay her head back and closed her eyes, dreading what the next few days might bring.

Tom's voice interrupted her thoughts. "I think you might be right."

"About what?"

"Someone's following you and the kids." He looked at her briefly, checked the rearview mirror. "That same car's been behind us for miles."

Chapter Thirty-five

Jennie awoke to stillness, a silence so complete she knew instantly she was alone in the cabin. *The kids? With Tom. That's good.* Whatever his failings, she knew the kids were safe with him. She wondered when the rain had stopped. Her last memory was of lying in the darkness, oppressed by the sounds and smells of an unfamiliar place. Rain had pounded on the roof, as unrelenting as the feet of an approaching army. She was flooded with memories of events long past, not yet expunged.

She got out of bed and saw the note on the table.

Plan on fish for dinner tonight. Or maybe not. The boys have on their heavy jackets and hats. We'll be back before lunch. DON'T WORRY. Love,

Under the brief message were three signatures: *Tom,* in his crisp straight-up-and-down style; *Tommy,* in proud third-grade penmanship; *A N D Y,* in the brave block letters of first grade.

She looked toward the coffeepot and shook her head, knowing its contents would be no more than lukewarm. *They're probably on the dock. I'll go down and say good morning, and then have breakfast.* Before she left the cabin, she checked the small bag in which her personal items were packed. The revolver nestled in a corner, incongruous among the pastel jars of cosmetics. *Not much help there.* She checked to make sure the safety was still on and transferred it to her jacket pocket.

A narrow path ran along the edge of the bluff and descended to the dock by wooden steps, sturdily constructed but worn smooth by years of use. A broken branch, a legacy of the high waters of spring, obscured the view of the dock from the first five steps. Between the fifth and sixth steps there was a small landing, effecting a ninety-degree turn in the stairs. As Jennie made the turn, she could see the dock, but not her family. *Where are they?* She started to move more quickly down the remaining stairs. A sound foreign to the environment of river and trees caught her attention. *A car?* She hesitated, listening. *Yes, a car. No matter. First I'll check on the kids.*

Wet leaves covered the steps of the lower level. Aware of the treacherous footing, Jennie looked down. The river, swollen by recent rains, pulsed, flexing its muscles, lapping at the narrow strip of gravel that served as a footing for the steps and the dock. Twenty yards downstream, the bluff jutted into the river at a sharp angle from the gravel bar. Jennie remembered how deep the water was at the foot of the bluff where the river had been forced into a turn. She gripped the railing tighter and moved as quickly as she dared down the remaining steps.

From the end of the dock, she saw the small fishing boat bobbing like a toy in the choppy water. Tommy spotted her first, said something to his father and brother, and all three of them waved to her. Tom pointed to the bright orange life jackets. She nodded her approval and waved back. *They won't catch any fish today. Even I know that.* She felt a brief moment of sorrow for them, shook it off. *Doesn't matter. They're happy just to be out on the river with their father. Glad they'll have these few days. Whatever happens, the family will never be the same.* She thought of the car she'd heard, waved once more, and began the climb back to the cabin.

Ellen, wearing a loose-fitting rain jacket with the collar turned up, her hands shoved deep into the pockets, was sitting on the porch steps, waiting. A folded newspaper lay on her knees.

Jennie said, "Shall we go inside?"

Ellen nodded and, together, they went into the cabin. She handed the newspaper to Jennie. "I thought you should see this."

At the top of the page was a fuzzy news photo of Jennie and Tom emerging from the church the day of the funeral, and just under it, a school picture of a very young-looking Robin, placed so that the three figures made a triangle.

"Sorry," Ellen said. "I didn't want you to come home and find this on your doorstep."

Jennie's mumbled thanks was perfunctory. She spread the paper flat and leaned over to read the headline aloud: "ILLICIT AFFAIR DISCOVERED." She read the rest of the article silently.

Ellen said, "I'd better go. You guys have things to talk about."

Jennie put her hand on Ellen's arm. "Wait."

"What?"

"Nothing." She had no idea how to say what needed to be said. *There's time,* she told herself and hoped it was true.

"You were going to say something. What is it?"

"It can wait."

"Are you going to be okay?" Ellen asked.

Jennie felt the gun in her pocket and nodded.

"I'm going then. Unless you want me to stay."

"No. We'll talk when I get home."

"When will that be?"

"End of next week. Late Friday. At least, that was the plan." She looked down at the newspaper. "But we'll probably be home before then."

Ellen turned toward the door, stopped when Jennie said her name.

"How did you know where we were?" she asked.

Ellen hesitated before she answered. "Tom told me. Why?"

"Just curious."

Jennie was reading the newspaper article for the third time when voices announced the return of her family. She folded the paper so the headlines were hidden inside and put it on top of the refrigerator. Her jacket was draped over the back of a chair. The weight of the gun had pulled the garment to one side so it rested on the floor, making the outline of the weapon clearly visible. She took the jacket to the closet and removed the offensive item from the pocket before she hung it up, then stood looking distastefully at the ugly metal object in her hand.

Tom's deep voice, braided into the excited chatter of Tommy and Andy, was just outside the door. *I have to get this thing out of sight.* She reached up, shoved the gun as far to the back of the shelf as she could reach. She closed the closet door and went to join Tom and the kids.

Tom took one look at her and asked, "What's wrong?"

"Nothing."

"You look—"

She stopped him from saying more. "I haven't had breakfast yet. I know you guys had some cereal." She paused, waving one hand over the rinsed-out bowls in the sink. "But it looked pretty cold out on that river. Bet you're hungry. Who wants scrambled eggs and bacon?"

"Mom, that's the best idea you ever had," Tommy said.

"Can't say I consider that much of a compliment."

"You weren't out in that boat," Tom said, crossing the room and laying cold fingers against her cheek.

She forced a weak smile and eyed the newspaper on the refrigerator.

After they had eaten, she put the boys to work clearing the table, retrieved the newspaper from its resting place, and said to Tom, "Let's go outside for a minute."

"Wait for us!" Andy wailed.

"We'll just be on the porch."

"Why don't you stay in here?"

"Daddy and I have to talk."

"What about me and Tommy?"

Both boys looked so forlorn, she said, "Tell you what, I'll help you with the dishes, then you can set up the Monopoly board while Daddy and I talk." She handed the paper to Tom and pushed him toward the door.

By the time she joined him on the porch, he had finished the article and was staring into the woods beyond the cabin. His posture was one of utter defeat, his eyes unnaturally bright.

"Jen, I'm sorry. I never thought it would come to this."

"We can't worry about that now. We have to think of them. We have to tell them."

"I know." His voice was a hoarse whisper.

"You're the one to do it."

A soft sound, almost a groan, escaped him.

"I've given the matter a lot of thought. In case something like this happened. I want you to tell them."

"Me?"

"You have to explain as best you can." She looked at the newspaper in his hand. "We'll have to show them that."

"Why?"

"If we don't, someone else might. I want it to come from us. From you. We've always told them to admit their mistakes. We can't do less ourselves."

Tom ran his fingers through his thick, sand-colored hair. "You're right," he finally said.

Later, inside the cabin, Tommy sat at the table, his small body rigid with concentration, using both hands to hold the paper flat as he read the words beneath the pictures. Andy, quiet for a change, watched his brother from across the table, waiting for some clue as to what it all meant. Jennie sat at the end of the table, between her sons, her own feelings put aside as she looked from one to the other. Tom paced the perimeter of the room.

"Why don't you take a walk," Jennie suggested. "You look like you could use some fresh air."

Andy watched his father with haunted eyes.

Tom paused in the doorway, raising questioning eyebrows to Jennie.

"Just fifteen or twenty minutes," she said.

"Okay."

Andy ran to give him a hug.

"Thanks, buddy." Tom's voice broke when he returned the little boy's embrace.

Tommy did not look up from the newspaper until he heard the door close. Then he said, "I don't understand. Why did Daddy do that?"

"I don't know," Jennie said.

He looked down at the newspaper. "What's illicit mean?"

"Uh . . . forbidden . . . something you're not supposed to do."

"That's what Daddy did with Robin?"

Jennie nodded.

"What's going to happen now?"

"I'm not sure," she admitted.

"Is Daddy bad?" Andy asked, finally breaking his silence.

Jennie spoke slowly, willing the unshed tears away. "Your daddy loves you. That's the thing to remember. No matter what happens. No matter what anyone says. Remember that."

And then they waited, killing time, for Tom to return.

Five minutes. That's what I should have said.

In exactly fifteen minutes, he was back. He entered, closed the door behind him, but came no further into the room.

"Did you find a nice place to walk?" Jennie hated the artificial cheer in her voice, but didn't know how to bring normality back.

"There's a trail along the bluff."

"I remember that," she said. "Why don't you take the boys? Show them the view downriver."

Surprised, he looked at her.

"The three of you need to talk. Without me."

The boys looked toward their mother, hesitant.

"Go ahead," she told them. "I'll hold down the fort here."

"Aren't you gonna come too?"

"Not this time."

Alone, she gave in to restlessness and prowled the small rooms of the cabin, anticipating, planning. Things were moving faster than she had expected.

Chapter Thirty-six

She went to the closet and reached onto the shelf. Her fingers touched only the soft shapes of hats and scarves. *It has to be here!* She stretched higher and peered into the back corner of the shelf. No use. The towering pines kept the cabin in half darkness even at midday. She switched on the light. There, in the far back corner, was the gun.

She retrieved it, slipped it into a pocket of her jeans, and grimaced as the hard metal edges dug into her hipbone. *This'll never work. Maybe if I put on a pair of looser pants.* She removed the gun from the pocket and tossed it on the bed as she went toward the still unpacked suitcase in the corner. The feeling came over her when she bent over. *Someone's watching me.* She knew it with absolute certainty.

"Hello," she called out, curiously unafraid, ready to do whatever she must. Her voice echoed through the empty rooms. What was that? She looked toward the window. Branches of a majestic pine moved against the glass. *It's just the tree.* Her mind racing, she bent over the suitcase again, removed a pair of loose khakis and slipped into them. *Why would the tree move? The wind has stopped.*

The feeling of another presence was too strong to ignore. She went to the front door, opened it, and looked out. There was only the family car in the graveled area at the side of the cabin. She went outside and walked around the cabin. There was no one in sight. Small gray shapes scurried furiously in the top of the pine tree. *The squirrels must have caused the tree to brush against the window.* She remembered the gun on the bed and considered going back for it. *Don't need it. Just squirrels.* Reluctant to return to the cabin, she followed the lane out to the road and looked for a vehicle parked along the roadside. Seeing none, she considered walking down the road to see what lay beyond the curve, but decided against it. *I'll go back for the gun.* She hurried to the cabin, hugging the sweater close to her body.

She paused when she saw the door standing open. *Did I leave it like that?* A flicker of movement on the path leading toward the bluff caught her eye. She watched intently. She saw a shape, its form obscured by movement of the intervening branches. The figure stood perfectly still, apparently not afraid of being seen. Trying to appear natural, Jennie went into the cabin. The gun was no longer on the bed. Nothing else appeared to have been touched. She sat down on the bed. *What next?* She looked toward the window. The pine tree, its branches now still, completely blocked her view of the area behind the cabin, including the path along the bluff. *Why am I waiting? I know what I have to do.* She grabbed her jacket before she went outside.

The shadowy figure was still on the path, a little closer to the cabin than when Jennie had gone in. Jennie headed toward the path and the figure moved away, toward the steps.

"Wait," she called.

There was no answer. The figure continued to move down the path, just fast enough to stay beyond Jennie's clear view, as though wanting to be followed.

"I know who you are," she called.

The figure stopped momentarily, then moved more quickly down the path until it came to the steps. There it stopped, turned and waited for Jennie to catch up.

They were face to face, not more than five feet apart. Jennie said, "You did it. Didn't you?"

No answer.

"You killed Robin."

"So you know. It doesn't matter. You'll never tell anyone."

A hand dipped into a pocket and Jennie found herself facing her own gun. "That won't help you."

The gun held steady, pointed directly at Jennie.

"Please. We're family."

"You didn't think of that all those years ago when you took Tom away from me."

"I didn't know."

"Don't say that to me!" Rage convulsed Ellen's voice. The gun wavered in her hand.

"But . . ."

"Since the day you were born, that's all I've heard. 'She's little. She doesn't know any better.' "

"Ellen, please . . . listen. That's not what I meant."

"What did you mean?"

"I didn't know you cared about him. I thought you were just friends. You even told me that."

"He would have loved me if he'd never seen you."

"But why kill Robin? Why not me?"

"I knew I'd never get him back if you died that way. But if Robin was murdered and he thought you were responsible . . ."

"So you killed her and tried to frame me."

Ellen nodded, outwardly calm again.

"Did you know about what happened between Tom and Robin? I mean, before I told you?"

"Of course I did. I made it happen. I got the kids out of the house so they'd be alone. I even put your old music on the piano. I knew she'd play it. Knew he'd come home and find her."

"But how?"

There was a jagged laugh from Ellen. "I've always known him better than you have."

Jennie stepped closer, drawn by the pain in her cousin's face.

Ellen held the gun up between them, kept it pointed at Jennie's chest. "How did you figure it out?" She sounded strangely calm, but her eyes were glittering.

"A lot of little things. When Goodley found my bracelet, I knew someone was trying to frame me. Mostly, though, it was Pynchon. When I saw the shed where he stores his things, how close it was to the murder scene, I remembered he was going back there to look for records for me. I realized he must have seen you in the clearing and thought it was me. He didn't really put it together until he saw both of us on television the day of the funeral and realized how much alike we look."

"Did he tell you that? I never knew for sure." The gun drooped.

"He didn't exactly tell me, but I added the things he did tell me to the things I learned from Emma. And Oz. That was the clincher. No one but you would have known that I'd see Emma's place and think of Oz." Jennie was edging closer as they talked.

"Don't!" Ellen realized what was happening and jerked the gun level.

Jennie stopped. "You didn't even know Pynchon. And you tried to kill him."

Ellen's face contorted. "I didn't mean for that to happen. After I heard that he'd called you, I went back to the flea market. Just to talk to him. But he avoided me. I didn't want to make a scene with all those people around. So I waited until he left and I followed him. I think he saw me behind him and got scared. He started going too fast. Then he started to drive on the wrong side of the road. That sharp curve. The tree."

"And you just left him there?"

"Another car was coming. I knew they'd stop."

Jennie reached out her hand. "Ellen, give me the gun. It won't help you. It'll be easier if you go to the police yourself. I'll go with you."

"No!"

"Tom will go. He'll be right by your side."

Ellen smiled at her now and shook her head. "You think it's over. You think you've won." Her smile broadened. The glitter in her eyes was feverish now. She continued to hold the gun level with one hand and reached into her pocket with the other. She held up a small cassette tape. "Remember the message on the machine? The one you thought you erased?"

"Is that the tape?"

"No. That tape is long gone. I made another. The final piece of evidence that will prove you killed Robin." She dropped the cassette to the ground and reached into the pocket again. "I have this too." She held up Jennie's missing cell phone. "More evidence of a jealous wife."

"It'll never work."

"I think it will." She threw the phone down next to the cassette, stepped closer, and held the gun to Jennie's temple. "I'll go to Goodley, tell him how I found the tape, confronted you with it, you tried to kill me, we struggled for the gun, and somehow . . ."

She really believes she can get away with it. Listening to her cousin, Jennie felt no fear, only a deep sorrow, regret for a lifetime of missed cues. Then the noise, so loud it seemed to be inside her head.

Chapter Thirty-seven

The sound, so loud it seemed a physical presence, immobilized both women.

Trying to understand what was happening, Jennie looked toward Ellen. Without warning, she felt herself thrown to the ground. Then, impossible as it seemed, more noise. Two short, loud bursts added to the continuing wail.

Shots. Those were shots, Jennie realized, and picked herself up. Tom was lying facedown in the path between her and Ellen.

He can't be dead. Dazed, Jennie knelt beside her husband. She looked up into Ellen's stricken face and thought again, *He can't be.*

Ellen stepped backward, still holding the gun.

Jennie felt Tom move, struggling to his knees.

"It doesn't hurt," he said, putting both hands to his chest. "I don't feel anything." He put his hand to Jennie's face and jerked it back when he saw blood.

Ellen threw the gun to the ground and ran toward the steps.

"You're okay," Jennie told him, taking his bloodstained hand in her own and soothing him as one soothes a child.

He looked again at his hand.

Jennie used her thumb to clear the blood from his palm. "Look," she said, "you cut your hand on a rock when you fell. That's all."

"But after I pushed you away, I felt the gun against my chest, and I heard . . . How could she miss?"

"Blanks," Jennie explained. "They were just blanks."

"Why would she have a gun with blanks?"

"I'll explain later."

214

They were shouting to make themselves heard over the noise, which still had not subsided. Jennie put her hands to her ears. "What is that?"

"I'll take care of it," Tom said, and ran toward the cabin.

Jennie turned to follow Ellen. "Wait," she called after her. "We'll go with you to the police. We'll explain." The words were lost, swallowed by the tumultuous din that filled the air.

Ellen was on the small landing when the din stopped as suddenly as it had begun. Jennie was on the path, just a few feet from the steps. Both women paused, startled by the silence, as frightening in its own way as the prolonged wail had been.

Ellen started moving again, racing down the steps.

Jennie watched, horrified, as Ellen lost her balance and, arms flailing, seemed to hurl herself downward. There was a dull thud when Ellen, tumbling like a ragdoll, struck the bottom step, catapulted onto the dock, then into the water, where the current swirled, eddying around her prone form.

Jennie was on the steps when she heard the childish voice yell, "Mommy!" Then Tom's, "Jennie! Are you all right?" She heard their feet on the steps.

"Keep them up there!"

"I'm coming down," Tom called.

Jennie was on the dock now. "No," she screamed, and then changed her mind. "Yes. Do. Hurry! But not the kids! Tommy, take Andy back to the cabin. Stay inside. No matter what! Stay inside until I come." She called the last over her shoulder.

The current had taken Ellen as far as the bluff. She was facedown in the river with the water pushing her relentlessly into the wall of rock.

Jennie fumbled with the chain holding the boat fast to the dock. "The key," she called to Tom, who was now on the dock.

"I have it." He joined her in the boat and unlocked the chain while she started the engine.

By the time they got to Ellen, the current had eased her past the bluff and was about to carry her downstream. Together they managed to get her into the small boat. It couldn't have taken more than

five minutes, but to Jennie, it seemed hours. She felt like the prover-
bial drowning person, seeing frames of herself and Ellen, a history
of their years together. *It can't end like this.*

She put her fingertips to Ellen's throat, searching for a flicker of
life. "It's too late," she finally admitted.

Tom reached for her hand. "I'm sorry," he said.

"It's as much my fault as yours. Maybe more. I don't know why I
didn't see . . . years ago."

"Don't. That won't help now."

"Maybe not. But we have to face it. Did you hear what she said?"

"Enough." His voice had a ragged, pained edge she had never heard
before. "I don't know if I'll ever be able to make you understand
what I felt when I came through the woods and saw that gun pointed at
you."

Her attention was diverted by sounds above them. "The kids.
How much did they see?"

"I'm not sure. Probably not much. They were fooling around.
And when I saw you, I sent them to the car. Told them to honk the
horn. Make as much noise as possible."

"So that's what the noise was." She smiled in spite of herself.
"Something they have a real talent for."

"Yes. I figured we might need help. And I didn't want them to
see . . ."

Jennie nodded her approval, looked toward the voices. "I told
them to go to the cabin."

"Go ahead," Tom told her. "You go to them. I'll stay here until the
police come."

When Jennie got to the cabin, a man wearing a red baseball cap
turned backward was sitting on the porch steps with Tommy and
Andy. A green pickup truck was parked beside the cabin. She sat
down beside them and said to the man, "Goodley had you watching
the kids, didn't he?"

He nodded. "When'd you figure it out?"

"That rainy day."

"How'd you know?"

"The way you acted. That and the fact that Goodley wasn't concerned when I told him someone was following the kids. That didn't seem like something a professional would ignore." After a minute, she added, "Thanks," and then, "Guess we better call him."

"He's on his way."

An hour later, Jennie stood with Goodley, watching the stretcher with Ellen's blanket-covered body disappear into the ambulance. "You thought I was the murderer, didn't you?" she asked.

"At first. Later, I knew you couldn't be. But all the evidence pointed to you, so I figured you were the key."

"What do you mean 'I couldn't be'? Why not?"

"I've been a cop for a few years." He grinned at her. "There were just too many things that didn't add up. Besides, it was so neat and precise. Didn't seem your style."

She chose not to examine his last remark too closely and asked, "Why did you have my kids watched?"

"I knew someone was out to get you and I couldn't be sure how far they'd go."

"Thanks. For that, I forgive everything else." She gave him a few seconds to ponder what "everything else" might be, and then asked, "And Tom? His relationship with Robin? Did you know about that?"

"Not until I read about it in the paper. I called a reporter friend and found out they'd received an anonymous tip. I did a little checking and discovered your cousin was the source."

"I wonder why. Most of the things she did I can understand, but what did she have to gain by that?"

"I guess we'll never know."

"Did you realize then Ellen was the murderer?"

"No. I thought it was your husband. I assumed you didn't know or you'd never have stayed with him. I figured your cousin found out and called in the tip to protect you." He held up one hand. "Enough questions. I have one for you. Why did you come up here with a gun loaded with blanks?"

"Oh, that." She shuddered. "With Andy around, I didn't dare have a loaded weapon. I figured the sight of a gun would be protection enough. Besides, by that time, I knew it was Ellen and I thought . . ." She was unable to finish.

"You're—" Whatever Goodley had been ready to say was cut off when the ambulance driver interrupted. "Ready to go, Lieutenant?"

Goodley nodded. He turned to Jennie. "I'll be in touch. You'll have to come to the station and give a statement."

"Today?"

"Tomorrow's fine." He nodded toward the porch. "I guess you want to spend some time with them." He started to go, turned back, asked, "How long have you known about your husband and the girl?"

"Couple of weeks."

"You should have told me. That information was too important to withhold."

Jennie shrugged. "I've got kids."

"Asleep?" Tom asked when she came back after checking on the boys.

"Yes. Finally. Believe it or not, I think they're going to be okay." For that, she sent up a silent prayer of thanks.

"How about us, Jen? Are we going to be okay?"

"Define 'okay.'" She doubted his definition would match hers.

"Will we ever get back to the way we were?"

"You know the answer to that."

"You're the one who says things always work out."

"The best I can say this time is that we start from here and see what happens."

WITHDRAWN